Nanny for the Single Dad

The Single Dads Club

Sierra Shipley

Table of Contents

Books By Sierra 1

Prologue 3

Chapter One 9

Chapter Two 17

Chapter Three 27

Chapter Four 35

Chapter Five 43

Chapter Six 53

Chapter Seven 59

Chapter Eight 67

Chapter Nine 75

Chapter Ten 83

Chapter Eleven 89

Chapter Twelve 97

Epilogue One 105

Epilogue Two 109

Thanks For Reading 113

About the Author 115

Books By Sierra

The Claiming Her Series

His Temptation
His Disaster
His Reward
His Challenge

The Rose Prairie Series

All books in The Rose Prairie Series are standalone set in the small town of Rose Prairie.

All Tangled Up
Tied In Nots
It Had To Be You

Interconnected Stand-Alone

Yes, Captain
Hey, Neighbor

The Single Dads Club

Loved by the Single Dad
Nanny for the Single Dad
Desired by the Single Dad

Prologue

Joanna

"We're letting you go."

Those four words have been floating in my head for months. Every day, the reminder flashes behind my eyes like a buzzing neon sign: fired, fired, fired.

It was never part of my life's plan to lose a job I dedicated years of my life to. Neither is the current path said firing has brought me to.

But this could be a good thing.

Maybe not right now, but I'm trying to be positive.

"Almost there. C'mon, we can make it." Dull pain radiates from my white knuckles clutching the steering wheel. My back aches in my hunched position, like curling up will magically make the car more aerodynamic.

The engine sputters and my heart stops.

It's only a short drive from Indianapolis to Briar Springs, but when the gas tank hovers on empty, it feels like an eternity.

For months I've been living on borrowed luck and I guess it's time to pay the piper.

Shame, and a smidge of embarrassment, makes up the ache in my chest the farther away from the city I get.

The corporate workaholic daughter, crawling back to her parents, disgraced and penniless.

Think positive, I remind myself.

Sure, I might've had to sell my extensive corporate wardrobe, empty my savings, and move back to my parents house, but at least I have a support system. It's just that not all of them know about it.

My sister, Taylor, of course knows. But my best friend Hazel? I didn't want to worry her, not now when she's in a love bubble with Grant, doctor sexy single dad.

I know that if I told her about this, I'd be sleeping on her couch instead of my childhood bed. But I won't do that to her. Not when I can't cover food or rent.

Tears sting my eyes, and I blink them away.

With the city long gone from my review, there's only one place for me to go.

Home it is.

Only when the Welcome to Briar Springs sign passes my window, do I loosen my grip. The sense of dread and growing disappointment doesn't ease up, though.

I might've exhausted all my options in Indianapolis, but coming back to Briar Springs might be what I need.

IT DOESN'T TAKE LONG to realize that maybe I was a bit too positive.

The summer sun warms my skin, the cool breeze offering some relief. People walk past the bistro Hazel picked for our Sunday brunch. She insists on continuing our tradition even when I can't pay.

"Still no job luck?" Hazel pulls her wild auburn hair to one side, keeping it out of her face. "I was hoping you'd've found something."

Same.

For weeks I've been going through the job-hunting process to no avail.

I shake my head. "I got nothing."

"And your parents?"

The waitress sets bubbling mimosas on our table, making my mouth water. Orange and champagne deliciousness zings down my throat in long gulps.

"Does this place have bottomless mimosas?" I examine the empty glass before setting it back down.

Hazel scoffs. "That bad?"

I really shouldn't complain. My parents are lovely people, they're just...my parents.

Reflections from the glass I'm twirling dance across the table. "It's not terrible." I shrug. "It feels more like I've reverted to being a teenager than a twenty-eight-year-old." As does the fifty dollars and the list of groceries mom handed me on my way out. "But I'm stuck at their place until I find a job."

Hazel waves over to the waitress, ordering more drinks. "Not even Jimmy?"

Growing up, I worked my way through high school and college at Jimmy Bean Cafe, serving coffee, pastries, and sandwiches. It was a great job, and one I'd be more than happy to return to.

Wind blows blonde strands out of my ponytail, whipping around my face as I shake my head. "He said he'd love to have me back, but with the economy..."

Even Briar Springs isn't immune.

The waitress returns with our second glass of mimosas, and we order. Hazel must sense my growing tension and thankfully moves away from my unemployment to less depressing topics, catching up on everything going on in our lives.

Diced potatoes fall onto Hazel's plate, her eyebrows furrowed in thought. "Wait, I might have an idea."

"For what?" I ask around a bite of my omelet.

"To get you out of your parents' house."

"As long as it's a job, I'll take it."

5

Hazel lowers her fork. "I don't know why I didn't think of this before," she says, more to herself than to me. "It might not be your favorite thing in the world, but it could work."

"The suspense is killing me," I deadpan.

She gives me a pointed look. "Don't be an asshole."

"Sorry, sorry. You're right. It's time to be positive." The fake smile I give her pinches my cheeks. "What is this magical job that I may or may not like, but pays money?"

Hazel slowly raises her middle finger, then laughs. "Fine, since you asked so nicely." She pauses, taking a sip of her drink. "Wells is a landscaper, and he's in the middle of his busy season, but maybe he could hire you."

My brow furrows. "Where do I know that name?"

Hazel sighs dramatically. "Do you listen when I talk?"

"Not when you're going into too much detail about what you and Grant get up to."

She ignores me. "Grant. Cole. Wells... My S.D.C.?"

Oh right. Her self-designated single dad club. Three — well, now two—single dads who are best friends and helping each other raise their children. Hazel met Grant, the Blue Dinos soccer coach, at her nephew Mason's soccer game, and they've been together ever since.

"Anyway, I think Wells could give you a job. I know you hate the outdoors, but this could work."

Hate might be too strong of a word. Aversion to the outdoors is more like it. I have my reasons, too.

In college, in true Hazel and Joanna fashion, we decided camping was our calling. Are we the two least qualified people to survive out in the wilderness? Absolutely. Hazel tripped over every stick, banged her knee until it was the size of a volleyball, leaving me to fend for the two of us. Every twig had a dangerous, life-threatening bug on it. The fire nearly singed my eyebrows off, and I swear we were being stalked by wolves. Does Indiana have wolves? I don't know, but they sure did that night.

But beggars can't be choosers. If landscaping is where I can get a job, I'll take it. Flowers are pretty, and I'm confident I could handle digging holes in dirt.

See, positive thoughts.

My fork taps against the edge of my plate. "What's his info? I'll call him."

Hazel tilts her head, her eyes squinting at me behind her sunglasses. "What?"

"Oh my god. You're serious? I was just kidding." She laughs, tossing her napkin at me. "I wouldn't do that to you. Can you imagine?" she guffaws.

I chuckle, unable to stop myself. "That's right. Laugh it up."

She dabs at her eyes. "I really think I have a job for you. I feel kinda dumb for not thinking about it before. Cole needs help with his kids. He's got Jett and Marie, and he's been desperate to find a nanny." She pauses, leaning in close. "A live-in nanny."

I let the suggestion simmer. It's not a bad idea. Like most teenagers, I babysat for some extra cash. Kids aren't terrible. I'd say I enjoy them if I ever got any real time around them.

Hell, I handled stressful mergers and acquisitions. I'm sure I can keep two kids alive.

"Okay. Let's do it."

Chapter One

Cole

How is it only Sunday afternoon?

As if weekdays weren't hard enough, the weekends seem never ending. Fights, tears, tantrums, energy. So much energy.

I'm not even sure I'm awake right now.

Taking a trip to the grocery store on a Sunday afternoon with my kids is the last thing I want to do.

The second we step foot on the sidewalk, Jett takes off through the automatic doors and into the grocery store. "Stay there," I call after him.

Marie holds my hand as we slowly make our way to the door. She refuses to be carried inside. My daughter is headstrong and fiercely independent.

The closer we get to the door, the more she wants independence. Marie wiggles free of my grasp, running inside to stand next to her brother.

Jett tugs on a cart, pulling with all his might. "I've got it, Dad."

A headache forms between my eyes, and I rub my hand across it. "I told you to wait."

"Sorry. I didn't hear you." The cart he tugs on refuses to budge. Metal screeches on metal as my son struggles, panting and grunting with the effort.

I grip the handle and tug. "We need to work on listening and following directions."

I've been putting off grocery shopping all week. I planned on ordering them and picking them up on Friday, but another angry phone call from daycare distracted me.

The daycare has a strict pickup policy. One that I've been struggling to meet. Mix that with the almost daily phone calls about Jett's rambunctious energy and Marie's tantrums, their patience is running low.

If I don't figure something out soon, I'll either lose my job or my childcare.

Feet thud against the metal cart, my daughter's angry cries echoing throughout the store. Jett runs down the cereal aisle, disregarding everything we talked about when we started shopping.

"Out," Marie demands, her cheeks red with frustration.

My patience is close to frying, so I give in. "Ask nicely."

Maire bobs her head, the shiny curls bouncing. "Peas?"

How can I say no to that face?

She lifts her arms towards me and I lift her up, saying, "Stay with me."

As soon as her feet hit the floor, she runs from the cart and grabs a bright red box of cereal.

"No, baby girl. Put that back."

My eyes slide shut and I count to five as Marie throws herself on the tile floor in one of the most dramatic tantrums I've ever seen.

Jett peeks his head from around the corner, another cereal box in hand. "Can we get this one?"

"You can only pick one." He's already tossed in a box with a baseball player printed on the front.

Jett looks down at the box in his hands, his shoulders slumping as he makes his decision. "But I want both." He has to raise his voice over his sister's tantrum.

I shake my head. "Not today."

"O-kay." With a dejected sigh, he turns around the corner to put the box back where he got it.

The creak of ungreased wheels turns down the aisle, and I internally groan. I don't need a witness right now.

A feminine chuckle cuts through the wailing, and I turn to find a young woman searching the aisle. Cheeks touched by the sun, blonde hair slipping free from her ponytail, and curves that draw the eye.

I don't want to stop looking at her.

She picks up a box of bland wheat cereal with one hand, a paper list in the other. Her gaze bounces between the box and my daughter, a secret smile pulling at the corners of her mouth. "You know, I think I read somewhere that if you join in, they'll stop."

"I don't think I've heard of that one." Somehow this woman draws a smile from me.

She places the box in her cart before moving closer. "Something about the shock of seeing a grown man flop on the floor knocks it right outta them."

We both stare at my daughter, her with a smile, me with a hopeless grimace as another screeching cry echoes through the aisle.

"You think so?" I rub the scruff along my jaw.

"I'd stop what I'm doing to watch that." She laughs and I find myself wanting to hear more of it.

I laugh too picturing throwing myself down to the floor. "I'm not sure I'm quite there yet."

She smiles at me before turning her squeaky cart around. "You'll have to tell me if it works. Same time next week?" she calls over her shoulder, her laughter trailing behind her.

I wouldn't miss it.

"CAREFUL." ALL THREE boys hold long matches, waiting patiently for their turn to light the end. Harrison waves around the lit end and

I automatically reach for his wrist, holding it steady. "Tristan, Jett, go ahead and light yours."

Wide eyed and open-mouthed in concentration, the boys light their matches.

Wells steps in, hovering over the three boys with worry etched along his brows. "Tristan, pay attention."

Grant laughs from where he mans the grill.

I point to the logs in the fireplace. "Put them here and then we'll turn on the gas."

Jett scrunches his face, doing as he's told. "Why?"

Marie claps her hands, her face pure excitement.

"Because," I say, picking my daughter up and pointing to the switch. "The gas will help the fire grow. Now Marie is going to light the fire so we can have s'mores."

Wells grabs the boys by the shoulders and moves them a step back.

Marie flips the switch, and the flames whoosh to life. The boys laugh, excited and enchanted by the flames.

It's the little things that make the stress of single parenthood worth it. Sunday evenings are one bright spot of the weekend. Harrison and Grant, Tristan and Wells. All of us together put a pleasant end to a long week.

"We are having s'more's right?" I toss over my shoulder to Grant.

After the interaction with the mystery woman in the cereal aisle, I spent the rest of the grocery store trip in a daze, trying to find her again to ask for her name. I was so distracted that I forgot all about the s'mores request for tonight.

Chicken sizzles on the grill. "Yes. Hazel's going to stop and pick some up." Grant's back might be to me, but I can hear the smile in his voice.

I'm glad he's happy.

Since he and Hazel got together this spring, he's seemed lighter. Happier.

I knew what that felt like once.

All four kids run around the backyard, enjoying our large yard. Soccer balls, dolls, and countless toys litter the green sea of grass. But it's nice to have a place for our kids to run and play while we de-stress.

Stress that's only going to get worse if I don't figure anything out soon.

That headache starts up again, and I rub at my forehead. Spots dance behind my eyelids as I will the tension away.

"Rough week?" Wells asks.

"Yeah," I say with a humourless chuckle. Balancing a busy work life with a crumbling home life has taken its toll. All it took was a year and a half. "You?"

Wells sighs, leaning back into his seat. "You could say that. We're getting busier and busier. We got a new contract with the city, so we'll be starting on that soon."

"Damn," Grant calls over his shoulder. "I'm thinking you need a night out. Isn't that what we decided?"

"We sure did." I smile at Wells' scowling face.

"No. I can't. Not with Tristan and work..."

Grant points his tongs at Wells. "Yes, you can. Hazel and I will take Tristan and you can do whatever your heart wants."

I smirk. "Or your dick."

For years, Grant and I have hounded Wells to get back out there. Of course, we all have our own drawbacks, but our friend is looking more exhausted.

Hell, we could all use a break.

Wells doesn't argue with me, which is surprising. "When would you be able to take him?"

I sit up. "Has the world ended, or is Wells going to take a night off?"

Wells lifts his middle finger at me.

Grant laughs. "I think he did. How does next week work for you? Hazel and I don't have any solid plans, and I'm sure she wouldn't mind Tristan being around."

Since Grant and Hazel have been dating, the two of them spend as much time together as possible. I know he doesn't want to force Harrison or the kids on her, but she doesn't seem to mind.

Wells and I do what we can to help Grant with Harrison, taking him on nights when he and Hazel want alone time.

We all look out for each other, helping to raise our children. I know I couldn't do this without them. Hell, I can barely stay above water now.

The gate clicks open and everyone stops. A head of auburn waves peeks out through the bushes, and Harrison takes off running.

"Hey, guys!" Hazel calls out as Harrison barrels into her, hugging her legs.

Grant jogs over to her, kissing her quickly before taking the grocery bags and leading her over to the patio.

"I won't stay long. Just swooping in to save the day." She gives me a playful nudge as she sits on the patio furniture.

"Thanks again for picking that up for me."

Hazel waves me off. "I do you a favor, you do me a favor."

Wells shakes his head, a knowing smile sliding across his face.

I look at Grant. "Should I be worried?"

He chuckles, shrugging his shoulders. "Don't look at me."

"No," she reassures me. "In fact, I think you'll be kissing my feet here in about thirty seconds."

"I'd rather you didn't," Grant says, pointedly looking at me.

I hold my hands up in innocence. "Not even on my mind."

Hazel laughs. "I have a solution to your nanny situation." I nod, gesturing for her to continue. "Well, I had brunch with my friend Joanna, and she's recently moved back into town and is looking for a job. We've been friends ever since kindergarten and I think she'd be perfect. She's smart, responsible, used to working long hours—" Hazel ticks them off on her fingers.

"Alright. Give me her number and I'll call her."

Her eyes go wide. "Really?"

"Yep." I hand her my phone and she types in my new contact. "I'm sure she'll be great."

She's gotta be because she might be my last hope.

Chapter Two

Joanna

The house at the address Cole texted after our phone interview looks like something out of Pleasantville. The white, two-story colonial-style house is damn near picturesque, with its red door and perfect landscaping.

This can't be it.

No, it's right. The text on the screen matches the house number and street sign.

Nerves are a lead weight in my gut. But I square my shoulders and drag my luggage up the sidewalk. Might as well look confident, even though I'm feeling anything but.

Questions race through my head with each step. What am I doing? Am I insane? Will I be any good at this?

Am I so desperate to leave my parent's house that I'm willing to move into a stranger's home and watch his young children, whom I don't know, all after a five-minute phone conversation?

The answer is yes, because that's all it took to have me packing my bags like it was an ad for a Disney vacation.

Here I am, two weeks later, moving in.

High-pitched children's squeals come from beyond the door growing louder with each chime of the doorbell.

Hazel said the kids were adorable, if a little energetic—nothing I can't handle.

The smile in my reflection of the storm door is tight. I look like a frazzled nanny, and I haven't even started yet.

Blonde hair sticks out of the messy bun piled precariously on my head, my cheeks flushed and shiny, and my clothes hang limp on my curvy figure. At least my pink tennis shoes look cute.

I wish I had something nicer to wear when meeting my boss. But seeing as my daily wardrobe will be leggings and t-shirts when I chase down kids, I figured I might as well get my new boss used to it.

A deep male voice shushes the excited tiny ones as the door creaks open.

Big brown eyes and a sweet face squeeze between the door capturing all my attention. Familiar curly brown hair and cherub cheeks have me squatting low to talk to the sweetest little girl I've ever seen. "Hi, cutie."

"Move back, honey, so we can let Joanna in." A large hand settles on her little shoulders, gently ushering her backward.

The solid red door opens further and I glance up.

It's him.

The very handsome, if tired looking, dad from the store.

The man I haven't stopped thinking about since that day.

He's young, tall, and attractive. Tufted brown hair hangs slightly down on his forehead, only drawing attention to his dark blue eyes. A light five o'clock shadow flecks his jaw, and I want to drag my palm against it. Like I wanted to the other day at the store.

This is Cole?

He seems to recognize me too. Different emotions flick across his face: shock, wonder, and one he tries to hide. Heat.

I smile. "I guess you can tell me now if it worked."

It's not something I normally do, chatting up frustrated parents in the middle of a grocery store while their kid throws a tantrum, but I couldn't stop myself. I've been blaming the two mimosas for my lack of judgement. And for leaving without introducing myself.

His lip twitches in a smile. "I wanted a demonstration, but you left too quickly for me to ask for one."

I laugh a little too easily. "Maybe I would've gotten the job on the spot. I guess now I get to test my theory out."

I'll admit that he's overwhelmingly attractive, not to mention single, but there's a big stop sign.

He's my boss.

No flirting. At. All.

He's got this charming crooked grin I can't stop looking at. "I'd love to see it."

Movement at his hip draws my eyes, and my smile, to the little boy with his father's eyes peeking at me.

"You must be Jett," I say, crouching to his eye level. "I'm Joanna, but you can call me Jo." His little smile blooms just before he hides behind his dad's leg.

"I believe you're familiar with Marie?"

"It appears so." Marie smiles at me, not as shy as her brother.

Cole offers his hand, officially introducing himself. It's warm and firm, yet there's something about the simple gesture that takes my breath away. I've shaken many hands before, but none of them have made my heart race.

"Joanna." My hand stays in his a heartbeat longer than acceptable, but Cole doesn't seem to notice. Maybe he's feeling it too.

"Please come in." Cole steps back, ushering me inside and taking my luggage from me. "Sorry about the mess. Things have been crazy around here."

The house is exactly what I imagined when I pulled into the driveway. Pearly white walls, hardwood floors, nicely decorated. Sure, there're toys tossed on the floor, leftover snacks and wrappers laying on multiple surfaces, but it's not far from what I expected.

"With two young kids, I wouldn't expect the place to be spotless." I give him a soft smile. "You have a lovely home."

Cole clears his throat, his eyes catching on the small signs of children living in a home. "Thank you."

"We have a big house." Jett seems to have gotten over the stranger danger in record time, no longer cowering behind his dad. "Don't we, Dad?"

I'm riveted as Cole chuckles, a crooked smile pulling at his mouth. "Yeah. One that never stays clean for long." Marie reaches for his hand, clutching at his fingers and yanking. "Did you find the place okay?"

"Yeah," I say, smiling down at Marie, who looks at me from upside down. "I've lived in Briar Springs for most of my life, but I don't think I've been to this part of town."

Meaning the fancy neighborhood. This part of town is the prime trick-or-treating stomping ground. I can only imagine what it looks like during Christmas when every house is lit up with lights.

He nods. "Grant said you're Hazel's best friend and grew up together. I've known Grant a long time, and he loves Hazel."

It warms my heart to hear how much Grant loves my best friend. For too long she went without it, and she deserves every drop of love.

"I like Hazel too," Jett chirps.

I lean down and scrunch my nose, crooking a finger toward him. "Guess what?" I whisper once he gets close.

His eyes widen and he cups his hand around his ear and whispers, "What?"

He smells like dirt and sweat. "I like Hazel too."

Jett giggles, covering his mouth. Marie lets go of her dad's fingers and walks right up to me, cupping her tiny hands around my ear. Her breath tickles and I chuckle, fighting the urge to pull away as she hisses gibberish into my ear. I play the part, acting just as surprised as Jett did.

Proud of herself, Marie walks over to Cole, who crouches down so she can do the same thing to him.

I've been here maybe five minutes and already I've smiled more than I have in the last month. Desperate or not, this is just what I need.

Marie and Jett go back and forth exchanging nonsensical secrets until Cole convinces them to take me on a tour of the house.

There's a woman's touch throughout the vast home, leaving me to wonder about what happened to Jett and Marie's mother. No single man would buy a house like this, at least not any that I've ever known. Pictures of the children line the walls, but I don't see any with a woman in them.

No wonder Cole needs help.

Jett runs ahead of us into each room, Marie waddling behind him. He's more comfortable with me now, and he's bouncing up and down with excitement. It's infectious.

"Bedrooms are upstairs," Cole directs.

Jett bounds up the stairs as fast as lightning. "You wanna see my room, Jo?"

"Absolutely." I grab Marie's tiny hand to help her up the steps. "I bet it's the coolest room I've ever seen."

"Me?" Marie asks, her big brown eyes glancing up at me before focusing back on the steps.

Cole follows slowly behind us, picking my luggage up as if it weighs nothing. "I'm sure Joanna wants to see her room first."

"It's alright." I give a reassuring smile, trying not to blush.

"So, my room's down here," Jett announces, rushing down the hall and inside the room. "It's so cool!" Jett darts around his room, pointing out all of his toy cars and robots.

"Oh, my goodness. It is."

"And here's my soccer ball and my Lego tower." He's like the energizer bunny bouncing around the room so quickly with so much pride that it's hard to keep up with him.

Marie grabs my hand, pulling me toward the door. For someone so tiny, she's stronger than she looks. "Me," she repeats.

Cole waits patiently in the hall, chuckling softly as his daughter drags me across the hall to her room. It's a soft blush pink. Very girly and delicate.

When the kids try to get me to play with them, Cole cuts in. "I think Joanna wants to get settled. You'll have plenty of time to play later."

They both pout, but don't put up too much of a fight.

The room they lead me to is larger than I thought it would be. Too many au pair movies planted the seed that nannies get shoved into a closet with a creaky cot to sleep in. But reality is much better. A cozy looking queen sized bed is made up in white linen and looks as soft as a cloud. Summer sunlight filters in through the curtains, dust motes flickering in its rays like glitter.

"No one comes in here." Cole says as my luggage bumps against the wall with a thud. "It's been a spare room since we moved in, so you can decorate it however you want."

Cole shows me the en suite, pointing out where towels and various toiletries are if I need them.

If I didn't know better, I'd say Cole's nervous. His fingers twitch like he's trying to find something to fiddle with. He slides his palm across his jaw, almost out of habit even though he's clean shaven.

Should I admit I'm nervous too? About this new job. Dealing with the kids. Living here.

But I'm most nervous about him. The way my palm still tingles from when we shook hands. How I can't stop looking at him—as an attractive man and not my boss. But most of all, I'm nervous about how my feelings for him, however new, could ruin this.

Cole's ushering his children out of my new room when he pauses. "I'm glad you're here, Joanna."

"C'MON." HAZEL LEADS me through the sparkling kitchen towards the French doors leading to an outdoor patio. "No one's going to bite you. But I wouldn't blame you if you wanted Cole to." She gives me a playful wink.

"I regret telling you anything."

It's nice that Cole invited them over for my first night in the house. After the tour, I practically holed myself in my new room unpacking. If I unpack everything, then it'll increase the chances that I don't fuck this up. But based on the look Hazel's giving me now, the same look she's had since we were kids about to get into trouble, I already have.

"Just wait till you meet Wells. Maybe he'll replace the grocery store hottie."

The nickname for my cereal aisle run-in stops me in my tracks. It's something we've done our whole lives. There's Already Married Randy, Tongue McGhee—I learned that one the hard way—Cowboy Hat Cutie, Exercise Rick...the list goes on and on.

"Stop it." I glance around the empty room to make sure no one overheard. Because if Cole heard it, he'd absolutely know who the grocery store hottie is.

Hazel pauses, one hand on the door handle. "Alright. I'm sorry. But just because I won't mention him," she jerks her head to the patio, "doesn't mean I'm not encouraging the two of you to get together."

I groan, knowing there's no stopping her.

Without skipping a beat, Hazel whips open the door, dragging me outside.

"Hey, guys. How's the game going?" Hazel leaves me standing just outside the door and plants herself in Grant's lap. They're so adorable with the way he pulls her face to his, looking completely smitten.

A baseball game plays on the screen above the fireplace. The volume's low, but that doesn't hide the numbers on the screen. It's almost pathetic.

"We're not talking about it," Cole mutters, lifting a bottle to his lips.

I have to force myself to look anywhere but at him. Every day Cole is tempting enough, but in a backward baseball cap? Someone's gotta put him in cuffs.

Nope, gotta stop that train of thought right now.

He's my boss, he's my boss, he's my boss...

Grant laughs. "He's just pissed that his team's losing."

The two men argue back and forth. Hazel gives me a commiserating look, waving me over to the couch beside her and Grant.

The three kids run around the lush green lawn like they have all the energy in the world. Their laughter reminds me of my childhood summers spent outside scraping knees and catching fireflies.

Cole's covered patio is more like an extended room of the house. The large floor to ceiling stone fireplace rests in the corner, the supposedly aggravating baseball game still playing on mute. String lights hang from above, the sun too bright in the sky to make a difference. Smoke billows from the closed grill on the edge of the concrete, the smell of meat making my mouth water.

A cooler creaks open. "Beer, Joanna?" Cole hands Grant two ice cold beers, passing one to Hazel before offering it to me.

Ice clings to the top, and I brush it off with the flick of a finger. The cold metal seems to burn my hand, but I hesitate to pop the tab.

My gaze darts between the beer and the kids taking turns on the play set.

Cole catches my moment of hesitation. "Have a beer. You're not on the clock, and this is your home."

Before I can open it, Hazel snatches it out of my hands, pops the tab, and puts it in my frozen hand. "Lighten up."

Ten minutes later, Cole deems dinner ready.

The ribs are tender and messy. In no time at all, Marie has sauce spread wide across her cheeks. Jett and Harrison only ate the meat, refusing the grilled vegetables, only relenting when their fathers made it clear they wouldn't get to play without eating them.

As we were eating, the sun slipped below the horizon and the fireflies flicker in the darkness. I've always loved fireflies. Something about their faint glow takes the ordinary to the ethereal. It's no longer a nice backyard with a green sea of soft grass. No, it's a magical garden.

After scarfing down their popsicle desserts, the kids are back in the yard kicking a soccer ball. I can't help but smile as Marie chases after them, her legs too short to keep up.

Harrison kicks a wayward pass, sending the ball onto the porch and stopping at my feet.

Jett races over. "You should come play with us, Jo."

I meet him at the edge of the patio. During dinner, the topic of the upcoming soccer season came up, and I mentioned I played as a kid. Not for long, but I played.

"You sure?"

Cole leans over his chair, his face soft. "Bud—"

"It's okay, I don't mind." I smile down at Jett's expectant face. "Ready to lose?"

Chapter Three

Joanna

Trying to get a toddler dressed should be an Olympic sport. Seriously, all Marie does is wiggle and squirm like it's a game.

It's a miracle I can get her dressed at all.

Sweat gathers on my neck from the exertion it took to get this little one ready for the day. She went WWE style and flopped all over the floor, with me chasing after her on my knees.

She giggled the whole time.

I've been a nanny for a month and already I feel like I've stepped into the middle of a tornado. No wonder Cole was drowning trying to stay afloat. I mean, I know people raise children alone while working a full-time job, but hell, this is hard.

I'm exhausted, and the sun has barely risen

"Alright," I huff, pushing myself off the floor. "All done." Both kids are dressed and ready, and we have...ten minutes to spare.

School started two days ago and I feel like nothing, no high-level meetings, no last-minute deadlines could've prepared me for the utter pandemonium of getting a five-year-old ready for school.

On. Time.

I unlatch the gate at the top of the stairs, grabbing Marie's hand. We need to get down to the car or Jett will be late for drop off.

"Okay, Marie," I sigh, bending down to pick her up. Let's get Jett to school."

She lets out an obnoxious screech, throwing her head back as her whole body goes limp. It's amazing. I never knew a child could transform into jello at the drop of a hat.

"No, no, no. We've got to get going." Apparently toddlers don't like being told what to do because she pushes my hands aside with an angry shove. "What? You wanna walk down the stairs?"

I've said the magic words.

Marie stops her complaining, picks herself up, and steps through the gate with a smile. An adorable smile that, in other circumstances, I would've loved.

Of all times to decide to be independent...

We're moving at a snail's pace. One slow step at a time. She's happy as a clam, smiling up at me with pride.

I wish she would move faster.

We finally hit the bottom, and I breathe a sigh of relief. Maybe Jett won't be late after all.

"Jett, grab your backpack. It's time to go."

A blurred streak of a five-year-old sprints past us, his feet clomping in rapid succession up the steps. "I gotta change."

I'm going to have an aneurysm.

"What? Why?" My neck pops trying to glimpse his perfectly clean clothes he put on not even ten minutes ago.

White liquid drips down his chest, covering his shorts, and pooling on the floor. Nervous blue eyes widen at my perusal. "Jett?"

His face falls, those eyes drifting to the floor in guilt. "I wanted some more milk."

It's hard to keep the frustration out of my voice. "It's okay. I'll clean it up after we drop you off at school. Next time, please ask for help." He nods. "Let's get you some clean clothes."

We barely made it to school in time. We were the only car in line when we came racing in for drop off. At least Jett wasn't late for school, so I'll take that as a win.

Once we got home, Marie 'helps' clean up Jett's mess. Milk is splattered in a large puddle in front of the fridge, his cup lying on its side in the middle. The empty jug sits upright beside it. It's clear that he tried his best to be a big kid and pour it himself, only to drop the heavy jug.

Then we settle into our new schedule of playing, cleaning, napping, and running errands before picking Jett up from school.

Having a routine is something I've tried to implement since day one. Their lives have been a type of controlled chaos, full of unpredictability. Having me around lessens that chaos.

It's not always easy, though.

I never imagined how much energy Jett would have. The kid literally runs in circles and bounces off walls. Marie's right behind him, struggling to keep up with her little wobbly legs and throwing two-year-old temper tantrums when she doesn't get her way.

Despite the exhaustion I feel in my bones, I love my job. It's different from everything I've done before, and it's so rewarding.

Seeing Marie's smile first thing in the morning, her hair a crazy ball of knots on the top of her head. Jett's sweet thoughtfulness when he draws a picture just for me. These moments make the craziness worth it.

After picking Jett up from school, we burn some energy in the backyard and have an after-school snack. Now, Jetts' school folder lies out on the kitchen table with stacks of papers for Cole to look through when he gets home.

"When's daddy coming home?" Jett traces the letter B with a blue crayon.

"Um, I'm not sure." Spaghetti noodles dance in the overflowing boiling water. Water sizzles, sloshing over the edge even more when I lift it off the stove and try to hide my muttered curse.

I'm not the best cook. I can cook, but serving healthy meals to two young kids and their dad was never on my life goals list. The food is edible at least. No complaints or untimely deaths yet.

Marie scribbles on a blank paper I stole from the copier in Cole's home office, the crayon I gave her scraping along the tabletop. "Daddy?"

"Sorry guys, I'm not sure." I lower the heat, double checking our dinner won't boil over again. "He said he'd try to be back by dinner."

Dinner that's almost ready to eat.

A text comes through from Cole saying he's running late and that he'll be here as soon as he can. I completely understand. Coming from that world myself, there were many nights spent at the office.

They both seem to deflate when I tell them, but they don't ask again. Even when we clean the table after eating. Not once as we work together to load the dishwasher and put away the leftovers, leaving a plate for Cole in the fridge. Or when it was time to get ready for bed.

Hazel mentioned that Grant and Wells would help with the kids on evenings like this, so I'm guessing this isn't all that unusual for them. I knew coming into this that it's going to be a process, Cole was clear about that.

With any job, there are bumps along the way to running smoothly. This is just a bump. There's been a handful of times in the weeks since I started that this has happened.

I can tell he's trying, though. He might still come home late, but each time he's coming through the door earlier than the last.

Except for tonight.

We're cleaning up the toys we played with in Jetts room when a door closes downstairs. The smile that crosses both their faces has one spreading across my own. In a split second, Jett flies down the stairs, Marie trying to follow him, only to hold her hands out for me to pick her up and carry her down the stairs.

The hug Jett has Cole wrapped in by the time we get there is tight. Cole's shoulders relax with his son's welcome home. Marie squeals and wiggles in my grip to be set free.

"Oh, I missed you two," he says, kissing Marie's brown curls as Jett pulls him into the kitchen. He tosses a polite smile and a 'thank you' my way before he's around the corner.

I guess this means I'm officially off duty.

It's been a long day. Long, but good. I could definitely use a shower—and wine—before bed.

The shower I take isn't a short one. Steam billows from the small room and into my bedroom. My skin instantly prickles as the water droplets still speckling my body cool.

I forgo my usual ratty mismatched pajamas for an oversized t-shirt and bicycle shorts. These are more appropriate for walking around the house, especially when I could run into my attractive boss.

Cole is everything I thought he was in that cereal aisle. Handsome, patient, caring. I love seeing him with his kids, playing and running around with them. Loving them.

It makes it hard to keep a professional wall up. It's so easy, almost too easy, to slip up and make a flirty comment. Sometimes, I look at him a little too long. Feel butterflies take off in my stomach when he smiles at me.

So I navigate around him like we're opposing magnets. He moves left; I move right. The last thing I need is for our hands to touch and set my heart racing when I know it means nothing.

Can't mean anything.

Because he's my boss.

The kids went to bed at least half an hour ago. Their rooms are quiet, the white noise machine slipping through Marie's bedroom door. Nightlights line the steps as I sneak down the stairs.

Commentators from a sports show play on the television in the den. The back of Cole's head rests on the couch, a hand raised as if resting on his forehead.

Several things happen at once. The floor beneath my feet creaks. Cole turns, the silent contemplation slipping from his features, and I freeze like a deer in headlights.

"Hey, Joanna. I thought maybe you were Jett trying to avoid bedtime." He gives me a soft smile that doesn't touch his eyes. Cole doesn't look like the happy man that came home lavishing love on his children earlier this evening. He's let that mask fall, and my heart squeezes.

I hold my hands up in innocence. "Not Jett, but you're spot on about avoiding bedtime. Thought I'd grab a glass of wine. I hope you don't mind, it's been a long day, and—"

"Way ahead of you." Cole raises his left hand. The brown beer bottle reflects the light from the tv.

Even though I've lived here for a month, I'm still learning where everything is. After opening several drawers, I finally find the bottle opener.

When my wine glass fills to an appropriate level, not at all near how full I want, I head back down the hallway, intending to go up to my room.

He's still sitting in the den. Leaning forward on the couch, his t-shirt pulled tight around the expanse of his back, head bowed. Cole looks lost.

It's not my place to step in and see how he's doing or what's bothering him, but something about this isn't sitting right with me.

Cursing myself mentally, I cross the threshold of the den. "Long day?"

Cole slowly glances up at me as I sit on the other side of the couch. "You could say that."

Red wine coats my tongue, the familiar tang and sweetness adding some normalcy to the situation. The commentators on the tv let out a stream of complaints, drawing my attention that I'm surprised as Cole says, "I'm sorry about today."

I shrug, taking another sip. "It's okay. It happens." More often than not, my work days in Indianapolis ran late into the night, so I know how it goes.

Cole shakes his head, sighing. "It does, but it doesn't mean it should." He takes a long drink. "Thank you for taking care of them." He tosses his head toward the rooms upstairs. "I like that they're at home, safe and taken care of. I'll work on getting back home sooner."

I nod as the silence falls around us. There's a tension in the air, and I get the feeling that he doesn't want to be alone. So I say, "This morning was crazy."

Cole smiles. "Was it?"

"Your daughter ripped off her diaper off and ran away from me. Thankfully, we were in the backyard. But man, she's fast!" I laugh, remembering the bright smile on her face as I chased after her.

Cole laughs too, a genuine smile crossing his handsome face. "Yeah, she likes to do that. The last time she did it, she tried to go down the slide." He chuckles. "I had to run across the yard to keep her from burning her butt on the plastic."

My tongue clicks. "That girl."

Cole sips his beer. "Aside from that, how's everything else going?"

"Fine." I try to ignore the way his gaze lingers on me.

"Just fine? You got any issues with your asshole boss who can't get home on time?" He gives me that crooked grin, and those damn butterflies take off.

I scoff. "He's the worst. Absolutely terrible."

"I'll have a chat with him. See if I can put him in his place."

"I'd like that." We're smiling at each other and I can feel myself slipping into that territory I shouldn't be in, but I can't stop myself. "He's not so bad, though. Plus, he's got the cutest kids."

"Ah. See, I knew I had some redeeming qualities."

"There's more than one, but I wouldn't want it going to your head."

The atmosphere shifts as our gazes meet. That familiar banter from our first meeting slipping through the cracks.

He shrugs. "It might be too late for that. But," he glances down at the bottle in his hand, picking at the label. "I'll work on getting back earlier. I'd hate to lose you."

Those words feel loaded. So, I nod, bringing my glass up to my lips.

We fall silent, sipping our late night beverages under the guise of watching boring sports commentators.

The last drop of wine slips past my lips. "Guess it's time for bed now." I stand, heading for the door. "You know, I think it'll get better. It just takes some adjustments."

He nods.

"Well," I suck in a breath. "Good night, Cole."

Cole glances over his shoulder, nodding. "Good night, Joanna."

Chapter Four

Cole

Having Joanna around has been great. And difficult.
Never would I have imagined that Hazel's best friend would be the woman from the store. My heart nearly stopped when I opened the door, and there she was.

First, there was the flash of relief that I had finally found her. Then came that simmering attraction I felt the first time I laid eyes on her. Only to be doused in frigid cold water when I realized that instead of asking this woman on a date, I'm her boss.

I almost fired her on the spot.

It would've been cruel and needless, but at least then I could see if that initial attraction could morph into something more.

Now though, that simmer is boiling. And I don't think I'm the only one that feels it.

Since that day several weeks ago, I've been better at coming home on time. We've fallen into a new sense of normal.

A normal we haven't felt since Camilla walked out.

It's been a long ass day sitting in meetings in penthouses of towering skyscrapers. Being a corporate lawyer has its benefits, but it's mentally draining. The only thing that makes it all better is walking through the door of my house.

Music plays softly through the speakers in the kitchen, the sizzling of a meal cooking on the stove and the mouthwatering scent of garlic drawing me in further.

"Good job, Jett. What's this one?"

Jett works on sounding out the word, his lips moving over the vowels and consonants.

I stand in the doorway to my kitchen, my son kicking his legs in his chair at the table reading off his sight words. Joanna moves back and forth between the stove and the cards on the table. My little girl bounces from foot to foot, dancing to the soft music.

The scene is mesmerizing.

Joanna smiles at Marie and joins in on her dance before sliding the sizzling cast-iron skillet into the oven, all while praising Jett on his homework.

Try as I might, I can't stop looking at Joanna. Her bright blue tank top hugs her curvy figure, her jeans relaxed over her hips. The golden streaks of her blonde hair glimmer in the sun's rays filtering through the window. It's down today, straight and swinging just above her shoulders as she dances with my daughter.

For a year and a half, I did my best to manage work and the kids, and it was tearing me apart. Run ragged by work, rushing home early in time to pick them up from daycare that kept threatening to kick them out if I was late one more time. We were living on takeout and constantly on the go, barely stopping for a moment during the week. Weekends were messes full of breakdowns and behaviors before a new week started up again.

Now that Joanna's here, she's a bright shining light to our day.

Also, a damn distraction. I tease Grant about Hazel and pick on Wells, but I haven't so much as looked at a woman in two years.

All that changed that day in the cereal aisle.

Joanna's hips sway to the beat of the music, snagging my gaze and holding it. A golden sliver of skin peeks out from between her waistband and her tank top, and I can't stop myself from wanting to run my finger along that tiny spot. Everything about her mesmerizes me. The way her finger runs along the paper of Jett's homework. How she pads from foot to foot to dance with my daughter. The curve where her shoulder meets her neck. The stretch of her lips as she smiles...

"Daddy!" The magic of the moment in the kitchen fades as Marie sees me, her smile dazzling.

"Baby girl." I wrap my daughter in a tight hug, loving the sound of her squealing giggle as I nuzzle her neck. Jett slams against my legs and I momentarily lose balance from the force of his hug.

The day's stress completely disappears.

The moment Jett's hands loosen around me, he's off like a rocket, stumbling through what he did today as fast as he can. We never expected that naming our son Jett would mean he'd embody it, but he does. He's wild and energetic and oh-so lovable.

Joanna listens, nodding along while she cooks and filling in the blanks of his story. "Did you tell him about your field trip?"

"Field trip?" I ask my son, reaching across the table to tickle his belly and loving his laugh. Joanna laughs too, the sound bright.

Marie wiggles out of my arms and I let her down, her little feet pattering as she talks her way down the hall, her babbled words unrecognizable.

I listen to all my son has to say about his upcoming field trip and the permission slip inside his tiny backpack, but Joanna constantly catches my eye.

Part of me wishes she would spend the evening with me after a long day. Have a drink like she did. Talk like we did.

It was the first time in a long time that I wasn't a dad or a lawyer or a friend. I was a man talking to a beautiful woman, loving her smile, and making her laugh.

Maybe we'd sit in the den, talk for hours about everything and nothing. Perhaps I'd learn what makes her laugh. What makes her smile. What drives her. Would she want me to kiss her at the end of the night? And would she want more?

But she's my employee. My children's nanny.

She's not that woman from the cereal aisle anymore. She's so much more than that.

I can't cross that line.

But knowing I can't cross the line doesn't stop me from inching closer to it.

Her hips sway as she stirs mashed potatoes, the shake of them locking my gaze.

I wonder what the sway of her hips would feel like against mine if I wrapped my arms around her. Would she lean in closer or push me away? Would she grind harder against my cock?

Jesus fucking Christ.

I clear my throat, blinking away the scene in my mind, and focus back on my five-year-old, taking over to help with his homework.

Once dinner's ready, we work as a team to set the table. It's hard to ignore how soft her skin is when our hands touch.

"Pretty paper, Daddy." Marie stretches out her little hand, an envelope clenched in her fingers.

Joanna apologizes as I take the paper from my daughter. "I thought I put the mail up high enough. Guess I was wrong."

"It's fine." I examine the envelope with its satin roses embossed on a cream background. "You're right, baby. It is pretty paper. Thank you."

"It looked important, so I put it on the top of the pile." Joanna fills their plates, cutting their meat into bite-sized pieces. Marie issues her excitement for dinner and Joanna laughs, picking her up and placing her in her seat. "I get excited about food, too. A girl after my heart."

But I'm not focusing on that.

I'm focused on my ex-wife's wedding invitation.

It's just like her to do something like this. Send me something out of the blue with no explanation. She hasn't so much as asked her mother to check in on us during our weekly phone calls. Now this?

"Cole?" A delicate hand brushes my arm. "Everything okay?"

The world comes back into focus. My children talk with each other as they eat, safe and content, and completely unaware, kicking their feet to the soft music filtering through the speakers.

Joanna, though...

"Yeah," I clear my throat. "Zoned out for a minute."

"Okay." There's skepticism in her voice, but she doesn't press it. "Hope you like your steak medium rare. I was scared I'd overcook them."

"It looks delicious."

Joanna takes her seat next to Marie. "I hope so. I followed the directions on the video, but there's a good chance I messed it up somehow. For all I know, they're raw inside. You might want to say a quick prayer." The serious expression on her face and the way she crosses herself lighten my mood.

"That bad, huh? I doubt it's terrible. But we can always have cereal."

Joanna chuckles. "Thank god. We might need it."

The air seems to crackle between us, and I clear my throat.

"Nuh-uh, Jo. It's good." Jett spears some meat on his fork and bites into it dramatically.

Maybe she's fighting the simmer, too.

JOANNA LEAVES SHORTLY after dinner.

Marie and Jett hug her tight before she goes, and she tells them she'll see them in the morning.

I'm not sure their mother did the same before she left.

Now that Joanna's in our lives, I'm able to spend quality time with my kids. No more blooming headaches or irritable attitudes. We simply get to be together.

Both kids are bathed, in pajamas, and ready to go to bed.

The three of us cuddle on the couch in the den. Jett rests his head on my shoulder, holding one corner of the book. Marie tucks herself under my other arm, snuggling closer to me. The book Jett picked out for tonight is bright and colorful and Marie marvels at the illustrations, pointing out her favorite parts.

Our lives are night and day from what they were almost two months ago. Nights like this were a rare occurrence, and one I regret not being able to do for my kids.

The stability we had before Camilla left vanished with her. Not only did my children lose their mother, they lost the only life they had known, and piece by piece I'm trying to rebuild.

I'm the only parent they've got, and I won't fuck this up.

There's nothing more important than this moment, my children safe in my arms as we read a bedtime story.

None of this would've happened without Joanna.

The farther into the book, the quieter the room gets. Marie slips into sleep and snores lightly. Jett yawns and stretches when the book ends.

"You ready for bed?" Jett nods his head. "Go get into bed and I'll be there to tuck you in after I put your sister down."

He yawns once more before disentangling himself from the blanket and slowly making his way upstairs. I follow his heavy footsteps, treasuring this quiet moment.

Marie doesn't so much as twitch when I place her in her bed. I breathe a sigh of relief that there's no bedtime battle before kissing her forehead and sneaking out of her room.

Across the hall, Jett's room is lit only by nightlight, his little body curled up under the covers. "Ready to be tucked in?"

He sighs. "I guess."

"Something going on inside that head of yours?" I step into his room, dodging the toys he didn't pick up, and sit on the side of his bed. He rolls over and I brush the hair off his forehead, peering down into the blue eyes that match my own.

He's quiet for a moment. "I miss mommy."

A knife slices into my chest, stealing all the air in my lungs.

We've had many conversations about Camilla during this vulnerable time before sleep. I always knew this topic would come up, but no matter how many times I plan for it, nothing could prepare me. "I know you do, bud. I'm sure she misses you, too."

"Do you miss mommy?" His innocent face pleads with me, pressing against my tender heart.

I don't want to lie to my son, but if I'm honest, there's not much I miss. It's hard to miss someone once they've shown their true colors.

"I miss her for you, bud. I'm sorry you have to settle for missing her instead of having her here."

Jett goes quiet before he yawns, rubbing his eyes. "I think I'm ready to be tucked."

"You are, are you?" I smile lovingly down at my son before placing a kiss on his forehead. "I love you. Sleep tight."

His little eyes slip closed and I listen to his slowing breaths as sleep overcomes him.

He misses his mother, and I wonder if Joanna's presence makes the ache that much worse. He's seeing someone who's sticking around, helping him like a mother should. It's no wonder she's on his mind tonight.

The embossed invitation and the handwritten note surge into my mind. I might not want to know what's in it, but my son would.

If it means a moment to reunite with his mother, should I be the one to keep that from happening?

Chapter Five

Joanna

Being a live-in nanny suits me better than working in a busy office ever did. Sure, it's taken time to get things figured out, but we've adjusted to a new normal.

Mornings aren't as crazy as they were at the beginning. There's still some chaos, but nothing like before. Marie and I enjoy taking our morning walk to the park after dropping Jett off at school. She runs and plays before it's naptime. We clean, play, and run errands before it's time to pick Jett up.

Dinners have been okay, even if there's an occasional mess or slight burning when I get distracted by the kids.

Everything's smooth. Great, even.

Except that I can't get over Cole.

My grocery store hottie.

The dark hair, the blue eyes, the way he always walks in the door with his tie loosened and shirt unbuttoned. It's even worse when it's been a rough day and his hair's rumpled, his five o'clock shadow shadowing, and his sleeves rolled up to his elbows. He makes it so difficult to not stare at him.

But it's more than his tempting appearance. He's dedicated, intelligent, kind, yet masculine in a way that has my toes curling just being near him. He takes his responsibilities as a father so seriously, coming home ready to dedicate his time to his children, putting aside whatever daily pressures he's coming home with to focus on them.

He's a man in a world of boys playing at one.

Jett's field trip was yesterday, and I had the day off. It was strange. There was no cooking or cleaning to do. No diapers to change or boo-boos to mend. I didn't know what to do with myself.

When they got home, Cole wanted to take us out for dinner. I couldn't say no when both kids looked at me with big puppy dog eyes.

The entire dinner was like something from a fever dream. Cole looked delicious in black on black, making his eyes electric blue. Maybe it was exhaustion from his zoo trip, but Jett was on his best behavior and Marie didn't throw one fit. Instead, we got to enjoy a nice dinner.

Well, everyone else did. I was shifting uncomfortably in my seat across from Cole. No matter where I looked, he was always in sight, catching my eye, and smiling at me. My heart was thudding in my chest and between my thighs.

By the time we got home, I felt like I either needed to take things into my own hands or douse myself in a cold shower. I spent the night tossing and turning, trying to decide if it was appropriate to masturbate while thinking about my boss, who was sleeping down the hall.

With his kids in the rooms next to me.

I barely slept a wink.

It's early, the sun barely peeking from behind the horizon. There's no point in going back to bed. Cole leaves for work soon enough and the day will start. So, I go down to the kitchen and wait impatiently for the coffee to brew.

My limbs are weak from lack of sleep, and I slump to the counter. I'm hinged at the waist, leaning face down on the cold marble. I didn't bother changing out of my silk, cheeky sleep shorts and top tank. It's far too early for anyone to be up to see me, anyway.

Cole usually leaves half a pot for me in the mornings. Since the coffee's still brewing, I doubt he's awake yet, which is good, because he's an early riser.

Once it's done, I can grab my coffee and sneak back up to my room, and no one will know.

A hushed squeak from the French doors has me winking an eye open. Cole's upstairs, right? He can't be...

"You're up early."

Shit.

The sound of his breathless voice has me bolting upright.

I've just given my boss a picture of my ass bent over the counter.

Fuck my life.

The tile squeaks as I turn on my heel. A sharp gasp escapes my lips before my throat dries.

Cole pulls his headphones from his ears, sweat glistening on his shirtless torso. I can't help but stare at his tanned skin, muscles, and sprinkles of chest hair. And there's no stopping my eyes trailing down to his shorts.

I don't think I need that coffee anymore. I'm wide awake now.

Cole clears his throat.

Embarrassment, hot, and humiliating twinges through me. I'm definitely going to get fired for checking out my boss.

To save some semblance of decency, I turn back to the brewing coffee. I'm glad he can't see my face because right now I'm mortified.

"I couldn't sleep," I mutter breathlessly, laser-focused on the counter in front of me. If I focus hard enough on the grain of the marble, maybe I'll forget how turned on I am right now. Or how I'm not wearing a bra and my nipples are tight and needing attention.

Such lovely swirling veins.

Veins.

Like the ones popping out of Cole's forearms.

Shit. Focus, focus, focus.

The refrigerator opens beside me, followed by the twist of a bottle cap and deep swallows. "I'm glad you're up. I wanted to talk to you about something."

Here we go. Here comes the whole, "You're doing a terrible job, so get out of my house," speech.

I think I'll take that coffee now.

Right on cue, the coffee maker beeps, announcing that it's ready. Thank God.

"What's up?" I ask as casually as I can while fixing my coffee. I've never been the type of person to drink my coffee black. If I wanted to start with ruining my day, black coffee would do it.

Needing the creamer, I turn toward the fridge only to come face-to-face with Cole's chest.

"Oh! Sorry. I, um, need the creamer." We're practically chest to chest, and I can feel the warmth of his body against my skin.

He doesn't step back like I expect him to. Instead, he casually opens the fridge without stepping away and hands me the creamer I keep shoved at the back.

I didn't even think he knew how I took my coffee.

"It's a sensitive topic," he explains. I suck in a deep breath, hoping to keep myself under control. "So I wanted to do it without the kids around."

Metal clinks against ceramic as I stir my coffee with a shaky hand.

Cole waits until I finish, taking the creamer from me. Our fingers brush and it feels as if I put my hand to a flame. Invisible heat scorches my fingers where his hand touched mine.

I just had to come downstairs this morning, didn't I? Now I'm more worked up than when I went to bed.

"Oh. Okay." I bring the steaming mug to my lips, needing reinforcements for this conversation. Cole has the same idea because he reaches around me for a mug.

I should not be feeling this way about my boss. I shouldn't be ogling him like a teenager or fighting the urge to know what his chest feels like under my palm.

Or leaning in to smell the warm musk of his skin.

God, I'm making this all so much worse.

He pours a cup and gestures to the patio.

I follow him through the French doors while trying to shimmy my shorts down my thick thighs. This is the worst time and the worst outfit to have a serious conversation with my boss. Granted, he's shirtless, sweaty, and wearing running shorts, so nothing about this really seems work-appropriate.

It's a cool morning, the grass wet with dew, the sky transforming into lovely shades of lilac. Goosebumps prickle my skin, and I cross my arms over my chest.

"Here." Cole picks up his discarded jacket from the patio furniture. "I took it off when I went running."

It smells like him, and even though I'm telling myself he's my boss, I can't help but feel giddy at the idea of wearing his clothes.

Cole stares into his coffee. His mouth opens and closes like he can't find the words.

This is it. I'm definitely getting fired.

"Jett and Marie's mother is getting remarried."

My eyes bulge.

Not once has she been mentioned. For all I knew, she died. I'm shocked that she's still around and I've not once seen her or heard her spoken of. Once a week they talk to their grandma on the phone, but that's about it. Cole's family lives a couple of hours away, but even then, no mom has been brought up.

Cole's mouth pulls up in one corner, making him look younger than he is. "Surprised?"

"Yeah, actually. I assumed their mom was out of the picture." I wrap my hands around the warm mug before bringing it back to my lips.

"She is and isn't." He leans back in the chair, and I fight to keep my eyes on his face. "She left shortly after Marie was born. She decided she didn't want to be married or have kids anymore, so she took off."

The sweet faces of Jett and Marie flash in my mind. It's been months, and the idea of leaving them for good really breaks my heart. "Wow."

Cole sighs. "Yeah."

My brows furrow. "So what's going on?"

He waits a moment, his eyes resting on my face. "She wants the kids to be there, and I don't think I should be the one to keep them from seeing her. Jett already misses her so much and Marie doesn't remember her..." his voice trails off as if he's questioning his decision. A hand runs through his damp hair before he continues. "The wedding's in Florida. If you're up to it, I'd appreciate it if you came along. We didn't discuss traveling as part of your duties, so I understand if you choose not to."

Flying is hard for anybody, but with two young kids? Yeah, Cole will need my help. Hell, I don't think I could manage all of that by myself.

"No, that's fine. I don't mind traveling. Plus," I smile, "You never know when you'll need my special tantrum technique."

Marie is guaranteed to throw a toddler fit.

His lips quirks as he huffs a small chuckle. "I think you're right."

My pulse races. We're dangerously close to flirting. I need to shut it down.

But it's hard to pull the smile from my face. I blink, willing myself to look away and clear my throat. "When do we leave?"

"I'll buy the tickets today. We'll be there in time for the rehearsal and leave after the wedding. We'll fly out next Thursday and be back in time for school on Monday."

I nod, the logistics playing out in my mind. Better to focus on that than on the man sitting in front of me. "Does Jett know?"

Cole leans forward. Tension lies in the lines of his face. "No, he doesn't. I'm going to tell him tonight. He's been vocal about missing her recently, so I know he'll be excited to see her."

He doesn't mention his feelings about this, but it's not my place to ask. There are so many questions I want to ask, but I remind myself that this is a job. Cole and I aren't friends. There's nothing going on between us, despite how my body reacts to him.

He's my boss.

I'm the nanny.

Time to focus on my job and get over whatever it is I'm feeling for him.

"SO, YOU'RE GOING ON a trip with him?" Hazel wags her eyebrows at me, a smile growing on her face.

Cole texted me earlier this afternoon, saying I was off the hook for dinner. Fall soccer season has started and Jett has practice tonight.

Since Grant's the coach, I figured Hazel would be free to meet for dinner. Which I'm kind of regretting based on the look she's giving me.

"You're ridiculous," I deadpan, ignoring her snorts of laughter.

"What? He's your grocery store hottie. C'mon, Jo. He's single. You're single. I don't see a problem with any of this."

"How about he's my boss?"

She brushes it away with the swipe of her hand. "Semantics."

"I never should've told you about this morning."

The moment we sat at our table, the replay of the encounter spilled from my lips.

Hazel laughs. "You know what? I think you told me because you knew I'd encourage it." She jabs a finger in my direction. "You want this to happen just as much as I do. I'm the devil on your shoulder."

Damn it. She's not wrong.

"Why are you such an enabler?" I ask with a laugh.

"Because we all deserve to get what we want." Her tone turns more serious. "Cole's a great guy. You guys would be good together."

I shrug. "I barely know him. He's attractive and a doting dad, but that's it."

"Well, I know him and I think you'll be great as a couple."

"On another topic," I clear my throat, "how's your sister doing?"

Her sister Candice and her husband announced their second pregnancy recently. It's a topic I know will get Hazel off my back about Cole.

She laughs. "I see what you're doing." She tosses her hands up in defeat, but her whole face lights up. "She's doing great. I'm glad they're finally telling people. I've known for months and it's been killing me to keep it a secret."

"Wait," I interrupt, setting my drink down. "You knew this whole time and didn't tell anyone?"

Try as she might, Hazel's not the best at keeping secrets. Her idea of secret-keeping is waving her arms in a crowded room and pretending like no one's looking.

She sits up straight and proud. "I did. I might've told Grant, but he's good at keeping secrets." There it is. I knew she couldn't keep it in. "She told me shortly after they found out. We're planning a gender reveal party here in the next couple of weeks."

"You think she's going to slow down now?" Candice is a notorious busy bee. I know I didn't have a lot of time when I was working in the city and Candice makes my hectic schedule look like child's play.

Hazel scoffs. "Are you kidding? I'm sure she'll be at work the day after she gives birth. She'll have no issues adding a new baby. Tony, on the other hand..."

"Oh, Tony," I sigh. How those two opposites got together, I'll never understand.

We've been so busy with everything going on that we've neglected our friendship. We text all the time, but the time we spend together is limited.

Hazel plays with the straw of her empty glass, stabbing the ice. "How do you like being a nanny? I know at the beginning you were nervous."

"It's great, actually. I love it." When I stop, Hazel gestures for me to continue. "Jett's a handful, but he's so much fun. And Marie is such a cutie. I love getting to spend time with them every day. It doesn't feel like work. I spent so long always going, going, going," she nods, "that this is making me see how important it is to slow down and enjoy life."

She arches an eyebrow. "Are you sure you don't wanna switch over to landscaping? We could make that happen."

We both laugh. "Don't you dare."

By the time we call it a night, we're both yawning, walking arm in arm through the parking lot to my car.

"One more thing, Jo," she says, brushing hair from her face. "Stop keeping Cole at arm's length on this trip and see what happens. I really think you guys would be good together. Grant's mentioned how different Cole's been, in a good way, since you started." I argue, but she stops me. "Look, I know he's your boss and everything, but take my advice. You might as well see what happens. You never know, right?"

The look in her eyes is pleading and genuine. Rarely does Hazel get serious with me like this, so I know she means every word. I sigh, squeezing her hand. "I'll try. But only for you," I say with a smile.

She smiles back. "You better."

Chapter Six

Cole

People bustle around us in the crowded airport focused on getting to their gate. It reminds me of how easy it would be for a child to get lost. Which makes me even more grateful for Joanna.

There's no way I would've been able to handle the kids on my own.

Somehow she's been able to juggle Marie on one hip and convince Jett to hold on to the luggage handle on her other side. With the competitive glances they keep shooting each other, I'm thinking she's turned it into some sort of game.

"Looks like our flight's delayed again." We've been here for hours. The screen above us flashes with another delay.

"What's it saying now?" Joanna sets Marie on her feet, checking to make sure Jett takes his little sister's hand.

"Another couple of hours."

"That's not so bad." She pulls out her phone. "We could get something for lunch and then head to the gate. I'm guessing Jett's hungry."

"Starving," my son adds helpfully.

Our flight was supposed to leave at 7 a.m., but has been delayed all morning. If we're lucky, we'll be on a flight by mid-afternoon.

Marie jumps up and down, her feet not quite coordinated enough to leave the ground at the same time. "I eat too, Daddy."

Joanna laughs, smiling down at my daughter. "I'm amazed she's not passed out by now."

If everything had gone how it was supposed to, she would've napped on the plane. But now she's fighting sleep with tooth and nail.

Dark circles ring Marie's eyes. She's done anything she can to stay awake. Throwing tantrums, pulling her hand free, and running away. Joanna and I have taken turns corralling her, giving her coloring books and toys to keep her busy.

I check the screen one last time, making sure that I have all the information before we leave. If anything changes, the airline app should alert me, but those aren't always accurate. Best to check everything now, so we're not running from one end of the airport to the other for last-minute gate changes.

Jett takes the rolling luggage from Joanna, dragging it behind him in both hands. He's been warned to stay with us, but I've got my eye on my rambunctious son as I grab the bags at my feet.

Marie lets out an angry screech from behind me. Joanna's been content to follow me through the airport directing the kids, but this type of squeal means trouble. Joanna shushes her before reaching down to pick her up.

"I'll take her," I say, stopping her with a touch to her shoulder. "Your arms need a break."

Blonde flyaway hairs frame her lovely face, the soft smile she gives transforming her into a goddess. For a moment, I'm stunned, unable to look away. I'm caught in her snare and I never want to escape.

Never in my life have I seen someone as beautiful as her.

Caught in her alluring gaze, flashbacks of our encounter in the kitchen rush through my head. Her luscious ass bent over the counter, the flush of color spreading across her cheeks, the hitch of her breath making her breasts sway distractingly in her barely there tank top.

I almost had a heart attack seeing her standing there. As if my heart wasn't pounding enough from my run, it took off like a stampede the second my eyes took in her form.

I was as distracted then as I am right now.

Her pink cheeks grow more flushed, that soft smile slipping into a concerned frown.

"Do I have something on my face?" With quick, jerky movements, she scrapes her face with her hands, working to free it of the non-existent blemish.

"I think you got it." I hoist Marie into my arms, holding her tight as she squirms.

It's not like I can tell her I was admiring her. I'm her boss, for god's sake.

"What are you doing, Jo?" Jett's eyebrows furrow as he watches his nanny effectively slap herself in her face.

"There's something on my face." She leans forward, sticking out her chin. "Did I get it?"

He examines her flushed face, taking his job seriously. "Um, I don't think there was anything on your face. I don't see anything."

"Good," she sighs, reaching out to grab the luggage handle next to her. "You better not let me run around with stuff on my face, got it?"

Marie settles, resting her head on my shoulder as I watch the quick exchange between the two of them. The closeness and familiarity between them shining through.

Warmth settles in my chest the longer we spend time together in the busy airport. Joanna doesn't complain about the long hours with two kids hanging off of her, and I do my best to keep my children occupied.

It's clear to see my children love her.

Since their mother left, I've done my best to give them the love and attention they deserve, but no matter what I do, it seems I fall short.

But having Joanna here? It's the best decision I've made. Even if I spend my life wanting someone I can't have, it's worth it for my children.

I'm not used to wanting someone like I want Joanna. My focus since Camilla left has been work and my children. It leaves no time for a personal life.

Sure, Wells and I made fun of Grant when he and Hazel first got together, but even I can recognize that our teasing came from jealousy.

Each one of us found ourselves raising young children alone. None of us envisioned our lives to turn out like this.

So these feelings I'm repressing for Joanna? They're getting harder to ignore.

All our interactions, from the cereal aisle to the kitchen and everything in between, there's not one thing I don't like. Not only is she beautiful, hard-working, and funny, she loves my children. That alone makes her the most attractive woman in the world.

The bond that's formed between her and my children is the kind they should've had with their mother. Except Camilla isn't the mother they deserve. Jett and Marie deserve to have a mother who stays, comforts, and loves them unconditionally.

Someone like Joanna.

Not someone.

Joanna.

They deserve to have her.

And fuck, I want her too.

Bellies full of greasy fast food, and our boarding time approaching, we make our way through the food court to the new gate.

Marie sleeps, drooling softly on my shoulder as I carry her through the crowded halls. Jett's sandwiched between Joanna and me, his hands clinging to the back pocket of my jeans as Joanna follows right behind him.

The further into the afternoon, the more people have shown up to catch flights that don't appear to be going anywhere.

"What's going on?" Joanna asks, her warm breath brushing against my neck as she tries to look over my shoulder, my son between us making it impossible.

Above us, in blinking red lines, the screen displays what I didn't want to happen. "All flights are canceled."

"Seriously?"

"Looks like it. Here." I carefully adjust my sleeping daughter and gesture for Joanna to take her. "I'll go speak with someone from the airline. Hopefully, I'll beat the rush of angry people." I look down at my son. "Stay with Joanna. I'll be right back."

Mobs of people flock to their airline customer service lines, and I join the throng of people grumbling about their flights. Luckily, the line for our airline moves relatively quickly, but that's about the only thing that goes right.

Frustration simmers under my skin at the long day we've had. Back and forth of flight changes and rescheduling, now this?

I walk back to Joanna and the kids, trying to calm down.

The crowd around the screen has died down and I spot Joanna's messy blonde hair and make my way to her. Jett sits in a chair focused on his tablet, his legs dangling as Joanna rocks my sleeping daughter.

Her hips sway distractingly, my gaze lingering longer than it should.

"Hey," I breathe, to not wake Marie.

Joanna doesn't stop swaying, her arm brushing against mine as she does. "What's the verdict?"

Jett doesn't glance up from the tablet, but I know his little ears are listening.

"No flights are going out anytime soon. Looks like a tropical storm is making its way to the Gulf Coast. Everything's grounded."

She nods her head, her lips pursing before she whispers, "So what's the plan?"

While I've had time to go through the options we've got left, there's only one I can stomach without breaking my son's heart. We either cancel our travel plans, which is unacceptable or...

"We drive."

Chapter Seven

Joanna

C ole's been quiet. I wouldn't say that's all that unusual except for the white knuckle grip he's got on the steering wheel.

It took another hour of waiting by the endless luggage conveyor belt to grab our checked bags and car seats for the kids. At least Cole decided against taking a cab to the airport this morning. The lines for rental cars were a million people deep and I'm not sure any of us would've had the patience for that.

While running around the airport wasn't particularly fun, I didn't mind it. I've found that my patience—once very short from working in a fast-paced business office—has grown exponentially since working with the kids.

I still get frustrated, but I've gotten better at hiding it.

For days leading up to 'the event', as we labeled it, Jett and I did a lot of practicing with listening. Not that he knew that's what it was for. To him, it was a funny game. Getting to do random dances, running around, playing dead, freezing... All practice for today and I'd say it worked. No nightmare type situation of Jett running off or getting lost in the airport because he got overly excited.

I'll take that as a win any day.

My favorite part, if such a thing can be said about traveling through an airport, was watching Cole with his kids.

After a short-lived nap, Marie was squirmy and ready to run. Instead of letting her struggle, Cole set her down and chased after her. Jett quickly joined in and all three of the laughing smiles were contagious. It made standing around much more enjoyable, and not just for me. People all around us, stuck in the same position, enjoyed the entertainment as well.

Although, I doubt they were feeling the same things I was.

The time we spend together with the four of us usually lasts the span of an evening meal. We eat, clean up, and then I dart upstairs or leave to run errands to give them some time alone together. So seeing Jett and Cole play and laugh with each other warmed my heart like nothing else.

Except for maybe the way he melts when his daughter wraps her little arms around his neck.

Or when Jett helps Marie color a page from their coloring book.

Okay, maybe a lot about this family gives me warm, fuzzy feelings.

Their dad, however, gives me very different, inappropriate feelings. Ones I shouldn't be having for my boss.

Something about a man playing with his kids is irresistible.

It's that feeling that keeps dragging me back to what Hazel said. Her parting words keep sneaking into my thoughts the longer we spend together. She has a point. I'll never know if I don't try. Hell, she's living proof of that.

Maybe I should take that running leap...

Cole looks amazing today, too. Even sleep-rumpled and exhausted, he still looks good. I've seen him in a business suit, and half-naked and sweaty in running gear, but jeans and a t-shirt? He's giving hot neighbor next door vibes and I'm here for it.

Women in the airport noticed too, and the pangs of jealousy I felt were hard to ignore. The only bright side was that Cole didn't seem to notice. If he did, he certainly didn't care. Which, admittedly, calmed the raging jealousy a tiny bit.

The luxury SUV Cole owns is silent as we put the airport in our rearview. Jett's energy in the airport has finally run low. He's fallen silent in the back seat on the edge of sleep. Marie hums so quietly to herself that I can barely hear her. It's only a matter of time before she either gets cranky or falls asleep.

There's something about being in a silent car that I can't stand, so I ask, "Not big on road trips?"

His shoulders seem to relax at the break in silence, his hands flexing as he loosens his grip on the wheel.

"Not big on days like this," he says, blowing out a breath. "All the rushing around for nothing, only to end up with two young kids in a long car ride, isn't what I planned."

I nod. "All the best-laid plans..."

He chuckles. "At least you understand."

"Yeah," I snort. "I would know."

He inhales through his nose. "I know a little of the story, but how did you end up coming back to Briar Springs?"

My involuntary sigh settles the rising tension in my chest. "I got laid off."

"Mergers and Acquisitions for Cooper and Pike Industries, right?"

I nod.

Working at the Indianapolis branch of the fortune five hundred company was a dream come true. I had just graduated from Liberty College and landed the entry level position. Eventually, my hard work and dedication paid off, and I worked my way up. But then a couple of years ago, things started going downhill.

Cole listens attentively, nodding his head as we speed down the highway.

"I'm sure you know the rest." I try to downplay how bad it actually got, but Cole's too smart for that.

"How long?" he asks.

"How long, what?"

There's something hidden in the look he gives me. "How long before you moved back? How long did you go without a job? Without telling anyone?"

Shame rips through me. "A year." I swallow. "I think I didn't want to come face to face with my failure, so I put up a good front. Kept meeting up with Hazel for brunch like everything was perfect. Lived in the same apartment that I could no longer afford. Until, finally, the warning sign started flashing and I couldn't avoid it anymore."

Cole's grip on the steering wheel tightens again.

"But," I sigh, "I'm starting to think it all happened for a reason." Marie's big brown eyes and Jett's smile pop into my mind.

"Yeah?"

"Yeah." I shift in my seat, turning to face him. "I love my new job."

Cole finally smiles at me. "So you enjoy the chaos. Good to know."

I laugh. "I thrive in chaos."

Those four words have his brow furrowing, and his smile slowly fades. "Right."

What did I say? This conversation suddenly died in its tracks, and I have no clue how.

A tense silence fills the car, and I shift back in my seat, left to wonder what, exactly, I did wrong.

HOURS LATER, MARIE babbles in the back seat as Cole pulls into a gas station. As soon as the car goes into park, Jett's little eyes pop open. "Are we there yet?"

It's been so tense in here that I can't help but laugh. "Not even close. Wanna go pick out some snacks for our road trip adventure?" I unbuckle, stepping out of the car to let Marie out of her seat.

Jett turns to his dad, letting out an exaggerated, "Please?"

"Only if you grab me some jerky."

Before Cole's done speaking, Jett unbuckles and climbs out of the door, reaching for my extended hand. Sometimes I'm amazed at how much energy he has, but then I remember that he's five. If I was five, I'd probably be bouncing off the walls, too.

The three of us slowly make our way through the busy parking lot. Marie tries to make a great escape, but can't pull herself from my death grip on her wrist.

Our first stop is the bathroom to change Marie's poopy diaper. Jett covers his nose, grumbling loudly about the smell. Marie, oblivious to the stench, laughs at her brother.

"Where do we start?" Jett asks as we scan the rows of gas station treats. The basket he grabs almost touches the floor.

Marie drags hers because she needed to have her own basket, throwing a fit until she got her own, her crocodile tears still drying on her cheeks.

"So there's two ways to go about it. We can start from the outside and work our way in, or we could go down the aisles and end with the drinks."

Jett thinks for a minute, looking just like his father. "Hmmm. I say we go straight for the snacks."

"Good call."

I follow after the two of them, fighting with Marie's grubby little fingers as she tries to snatch every item within reach.

The bell dings and Cole steps in. Even though I've been with him all day, I can't help but have butterflies.

"I've got 'em," he says, a hand landing on my lower back.

This small touch has goosebumps peppering my skin. Does he know what he's doing to me?

I nod, reveling in the feel of his hand sliding down my back as I head towards the restroom. It's an innocent touch, yet it feels like something more.

Or I'm just reading into things.

Gone is the quiet drive. Snack bags crinkle, the kids chatter, and the speakers play kid music. I'm longing for the quiet now.

The convivial atmosphere quickly dies out as their confinement to their seats sets in. I'd been prepared for a much shorter plane ride, but a road trip? I try everything I can think of to keep them entertained.

Marie's not having any of it. She lets out a piercing wail that has Jett covering his ears. Cole tries his best to cajole her as he drives, but nothing helps.

"We can pull over at the next exit," Cole says over the screaming from the back seat. My neck hurts from contorting myself from the front seat to calm her down and though my patience has grown, there's only so much of a screaming toddler any person can take.

"Let me try something," I offer, unclipping my seatbelt.

I can feel Cole's bewildered gaze on my back as I shimmy up to my knees, ducking my head to keep from knocking it on the roof.

"What are you doing?"

"This isn't as easy as I remember it being," I huff, trying to keep my balance as I crawl up onto the center console.

The top of Cole's head bobs between the road and where I'm struggling. "Joanna."

I'm pretty certain Cole gets well acquainted with my ass, but desperate times call for desperate measures.

With a grunt, I push myself up, angling my shoulders between the narrow opening, smiling at Jett in victory. "Here I come."

Jett laughs, tossing his head back with amusement.

Bracing my hands on the headrests, I shove once more. But, I don't move. My large ass hips are stuck between the front seats.

The scene from Peter Pan where Tinker Bell tries to fit through the keyhole comes to mind.

The car fills with my and Jett's laughter. I dare-say I even hear Cole's deep rumble, too.

"I think I'm stuck," I laugh.

"I've got you, Jo!" Jett laughs hysterically, sweetly grabbing my hand and tugging me to the back after I tilt my hips to slide through.

Red-faced and a little winded, I plop between Jett and Marie, only a tad squished by the car seats. Marie's dark brows furrow, her eyes wide with surprise and dripping with tears. "Well, hi."

Cole laughs at me from the front seat, his eyes catching mine in the rearview. "A little warning next time. You gotta prepare a guy for a surprise like that. I almost ran us off the road."

"What? You don't enjoy an element of surprise?" I brush strands of hair from my flushed face.

Cole's eyes burn into mine. "I didn't say I didn't enjoy it."

Holy hell.

So often I try to stay out of his way, keep my head down, push thoughts of him away, and do my job. But with today and all the craziness we've dealt with, things are shifting.

In what way, I'm not exactly sure, but there's plenty of time to figure it out.

Chapter Eight

Cole

Soft snores and heavy breathing threaten to lull me to sleep. White lines streak by, my only view on the empty night swept highway. It's well past midnight and the day of travel is taking its toll.

We've made several stops on our unplanned trip so everyone could stretch their legs and kill some energy. But mine has been slowly draining.

The only thing keeping my mind occupied is thoughts of Joanna.

She's been helpful, but absolutely distracting. I damn near had a heart attack when her ass landed in my face. Those leggings leave nothing to the imagination, and I can damn well imagine scenarios I shouldn't be.

From where she was sitting in the back seat between my two children, I had the perfect view of her face. Every expression, every smile, every laugh drew my eyes to her.

Even now as she sleeps, the lights from the dash hitting her face, I can't stop glancing at her. Her full lips are parted slightly and the thought of her lips against mine leaves me with longing to make that thought come true.

I've kept the music low to keep from disturbing their peaceful sleeping, but my eyes grow heavier with each passing second.

Joanna offered to drive many times, but I'm responsible for this trip and she certainly didn't sign up to drive for hours at a time.

But I can't deny that it's more difficult to open my eyes with each blink. Trying to keep sleep from pulling me under, I scrape a hand down my stubbled face and slap my cheeks; the sound like a thunderclap.

Joanna moans in her sleep, her weight shifting on the seat as she lifts her head. She yawns and I can't stop myself from yawning with her.

Joanna snickers, her eyes sliding over to mine. "Tired?"

There's no point in trying to hide it. "Yeah. It's getting hard to stay awake."

She nods. "Pull over at the next exit. I'll drive so you can get some sleep." She leans forward to the built-in GPS on the dash, scrolling until she finds the next gas station. "We can get gas and switch drivers, and I can grab myself some caffeine."

The stubbornness in me wants to protest. In the end, logic and general safety beat it down.

"Thanks," I sigh.

"Wow," she smiles. "I thought I would've gotten more of a struggle. I'm surprised."

"Just keeping you on your toes," I joke, fighting off another yawn.

It doesn't take long until we see the lights of the nearest gas station, and I pull off the highway.

Humid air fills the cabin as Joanna steps out. We're getting closer to the incoming storm that grounded our flight. With each stop, I've checked its trajectory, so we should only hit mild weather.

"Do you want anything from inside?" Joanna stretches her arms over her head, her shirt sliding up to reveal a sliver of skin.

Every minuscule movement, her hair floating with the evening breeze, the curve of her waist flaring out to her hips, draws me into a trance. I knew having her come on this trip would be a test of temptation, but now it's almost unbearable.

"What?"

She lowers her arms, her blue eyes slipping open. "You want anything?"

That sliver of skin quickly gets covered as she tugs her shirt down as if embarrassed.

"Some water would be great. Thanks."

Water to help me recover from the dry mouth I got while looking at her.

How in the hell am I supposed to survive the rest of this trip?

LIGHT FILTERS THROUGH my closed eyelids, my body rocking gently as the car speeds down the highway. Music, a familiar melody I can't quite place, grows louder.

It's still early morning, the sun not yet slipping above the horizon. Rain drops splatter quietly against the windshield, the dull thud of the wipers melding with the music.

I'm not sure what woke me up from a dead sleep, but I'm quickly figuring it out.

A near-empty bottle crinkles as Joanna twists the bottle cap tight before dropping it into the cup holder. Her head bobs with the music, her eyes darting to the back seat before slipping over to me where I pretend to be sleeping.

She looks like she's up to something and I want to find out.

All it takes is a quick reach of a hand to adjust the volume.

Bohemian Rhapsody.

Joanna joins the slow beginning of the song, her arms floating in the air like she's conducting. Her voice might be a bit pitchy, but I'll give her an exception since she's trying to stay quiet.

I snort when she starts to play her air guitar. The fingers of her right hand strum while her left play make believe notes. I'm blatantly watching her now. Gone is all pretense of sleep. This is a show I don't want to miss, and there's no way I'm letting her stop.

It's hard to contain my laughter when she tries to sing every part of the Opera section. She's completely lost to the music, oblivious to everything except the song and the long stretch of road ahead of us.

My favorite part? I never pictured Joanna as a rocker chick, but she's got a killer headbanging session going on. In time with the beat, Joanna bobs her head, the bun bouncing messily on her head.

Even winded from her quiet concert she manages to finish strong. Her small hand reaches toward the windshield as the music fades out.

The expression on her face when I clap is one I'll never forget. "That was the best thing I've ever seen."

Roaring laughter doubles me over, my sides splitting from trying to keep quiet.

Joanna's eyes widen and her mouth drops open. "You. Saw. Nothing."

Tears pool in the corners of my eyes and I wipe them away with the flick of a hand. "I'm impressed."

Her stern expression softens, her embarrassment giving way to chuckles. "Shut up. How long were you watching me? I swear you were asleep."

She looks over her shoulder making sure she didn't wake anyone else.

Remembering the kids in the backseat, I lower my voice. "The whole time."

She gasps. "You did not."

"I'm not complaining. Any other concert-inducing songs I need to be aware of? I'd hate to miss the next performance."

"Stop." I love hearing her laugh. It's so free and lighthearted that I can't wait to hear it again. "I can't believe you were watching me." She shakes her head in disbelief. "If I hear another performance-worthy song come on, I'll be sure to let you know."

We smile at each other in the dark cabin of the car. I haven't felt this feeling in a long time. It's like I'm slowly inching up to the top of the rollercoaster, my stomach fluttering, full of excitement and anticipation of what's to come.

"I look forward to it."

I can feel Joanna's eyes flicking over to me the longer we drive. There's no way I'm falling back asleep and part of me knows it's because I want to get to know her more.

She turns toward me, biting her lip. It's clear she wants to ask a question, but is stopping herself.

"What?"

"Please tell me if I'm overstepping here, but what's the story with their mom?" She glances into the back seat. "They don't talk about her, you don't mention her, and there aren't really any pictures of her in the house." I open my mouth to answer, but she rushes out, "No, sorry, please don't answer that. It's none of my business."

Camilla isn't a topic I enjoy discussing. It took time for the sting of her loss to heal, even if there's still some anger.

Joanna deserves to know. I want her to know. Especially after hearing about how she took care of herself, not letting anyone in about her situation for a year. I want her to know something about me. Want her to see this part of my past like I did hers.

"Camilla and I got married after she got pregnant with Jett. Looking back, she always had one foot out of the door. It's that wildness that drew me to her." I suck in a deep breath. "I worked hard and kept my head down trying to keep her happy. Got us a nice apartment in the city. Then she got pregnant with Marie and we made the move to the suburbs. It was the beginning of the end."

I didn't see it then, but she thrived in the chaos, too. Looked for it anywhere she could get it.

When Joanna mentioned it, it reminded me too much of Camilla. But Joanna isn't Camilla. She's something entirely unique.

"What happened?" Joanna asks softly.

"She left. Dropped Jett off at pre-school and left Marie at Grant's office." Her eyes widen, darting between me and the road. "I didn't find out until Grant called me, and by then, she was already gone. Packed up her bags and walked right out of the door."

The words hang heavy between us.

"I don't know what to say." Her voice is heavy with sadness.

"I got the divorce papers the next week." I press on, wanting her to know everything, like how I want to know everything about her. "She'd been planning it for a while."

Joanna's voice is soft. "I'm sorry."

Those two simple words ease any sting I might still have. I was heartbroken, confused, stunned. Struggling to pick up the broken pieces of my family.

But that's the past now. The pieces are mended, glued together in a gilded mosaic and resting in the hands of the woman next to me.

The woman I want to be my future.

I shake my head. "What I can't understand, or even forgive, is that she left them." I turn in my seat, looking back at my sleeping children. Jett's mouth gapes open, drool creeping down the corner. Marie's heart-shaped lips are parted slightly, her breathing deep and even. "They don't understand why she left. Hell, Marie doesn't even remember her. But Jett does."

Joanna shakes her head as if in disbelief. "She just left them?" Her eyes dart to the rearview mirror. "How could she leave them?"

Even though she asks the question out loud, it feels like she's asking herself.

"I've asked myself the same thing. She denied custody at every turn. Gave them up without so much as a fight."

Thoughtful silence falls between us.

"So why are we going to her wedding? If they don't know her, why go through all this trouble?"

That's what's been plaguing me this entire trip.

I push my hand through my hair and sigh. "What good would it do to keep them from her?"

Joanna's brow furrows. "I don't understand."

Empty laughter springs from my mouth. "Sometimes I don't either."

"Talk me through it, then. Maybe we'll both understand." Joanna reaches across the console and squeezes my hand. The small gesture is reassuring and intimate. And over far too quickly.

It's been so long since I've had someone to talk like this with. Bare my secrets and thoughts to. Wells and Grant are good sounding boards, but it's not the same as this. Not as deep.

"No matter what she did, or how angry I am, she's their mother. Jett's old enough to remember her. Ask about her. Miss her. Am I willing to be the kind of parent who keeps their kids away from their mother? This could be the only time, the only chance. My children deserve that much."

Joanna sighs, nodding. "So we're going to Florida."

I nod. "We're going to Florida."

Rain droplets splatter on the windshield, the rain growing stronger with each passing mile.

Joanna sucks in a breath, looking nervously over at me. There's a sparkle in her eyes, though. "Do I need to be on high alert to make sure we don't have a kidnapping on our hands? I've got some killer throat-punching skills."

There she goes again, making me laugh when I least expect it. "I don't think that will be a problem." I chuckle again, shaking my head. "Throat punching skills?"

She flashes a brilliant smile. "I took some self-defense classes several years ago. Pretty sure I could take her."

It's amazing how she can turn everything around. Hell, she's been doing it since the day we met in the grocery store. She swoops in and makes everything right again.

I shake my head in disbelief at this woman. "I don't doubt it. But on the off chance you do, I know a good lawyer."

Joanna laughs. "You do, do you? You know, I have very specific specifications for my lawyer. Might make it difficult."

"How specific are we talking?"

"Oh, I was thinking someone tall, maybe six-two-ish. Easy on the eyes. Willing to go above and beyond for the people he cares about. With two adorable kids and the best damn nanny in the world. Know anyone like that?"

I hum, scraping my hand along my chin. "Only one person comes to mind."

Chapter Nine

Joanna

"Fancy seeing you here." Cole's deep voice sends chills down my spine. Even after hours of talking in the car, it still has the same effect on me.

The hotel's continental breakfast room has far too many people for my liking. Especially before coffee.

It was close to four in the morning when we pulled into the parking lot of the nicest hotel I've ever seen. Bound and determined to make it inside in one trip, we each loaded up—him with Jett, me with Marie—dragging our bags behind us. I didn't bother locking the door to the adjoining room before stripping down into my underwear and crawling into bed.

Familiar butterflies swoop in my stomach. "You feeling bright-eyed and bushy-tailed, too?" For the first time in hours, I look up at him.

Good God, he still looks amazing.

I've got giant bags under my eyes the size of Alaska and his five-o'clock shadow makes him look like a hero from a romance novel.

Go figure.

He stifles a yawn. "Never felt better."

I laugh, stirring my coffee with a flimsy swizzle stick. He might look delicious, but at least he feels like shit warmed over, too.

Misery loves company and all.

Little hands wave from behind Cole's shoulder and I lean around him, trying to keep my distance. After talking and flirting with Cole last night, the last thing I need is to be close to him.

Jett sits on his knees at a table, strawberry jam streaked across his cheek. I wiggle my fingers back at him, scrunching my nose in our typical morning greeting.

I don't have time to register that Marie's nowhere to be found before she sneak attacks me. Teleporting out of nowhere from behind her father's legs, Marie plows straight into my knees wrapping her arms around me like a vise.

Coffee sloshes over the brim of the flimsy hotel cup scalding my fingers. Which helps distract me from the fact that I've practically fallen into Cole's waiting arms.

Being in his arms eclipses everything.

Blood rushes straight to my head, whooshing through my eardrums in a deafening pattern that, funnily enough, matches the squeeze of Cole's fingers on my waist.

If it weren't for the coffee burning my fingers, the two-year-old clinging to my legs, and the general situation as a whole, this might be the foot-popping type of moment Mia Thermopolis was constantly going on about.

My skin still vibrates from the feeling of Cole's hands on me as I'm set back on my feet, napkins pressed to my burned hand.

Pain surpasses the feeling of Cole's arms, the sting from my fingers shoved back to the forefront. I curse quietly, setting the steaming cup on the counter to look at the damage.

The four fingers on my right hand are splotched red from where the coffee splattered, but it's nothing serious. I've been burned worse from my nightly showers. Sure, it's tender, but once I stop focusing on the sting and think about the fact that I was in Cole's arms, I won't even notice it.

On instinct, I flex my hand.

Cole's gentle but firm fingers wrap around my wrist. "Is it bad?"

Honestly? I can't feel a damn thing. Not with his skin against mine.

"No, it's fine." I clear my throat and try to pull my hand free, but he doesn't let me out of his grasp. "Really."

Small hands tug at my leg. Marie has one hand fisted on her dad's shorts and the other gripping the fabric of my pants. "Hurt?"

I suck in a hissed breath as Cole runs ice against my overheated fingers.

"Yes, honey, Joanna's hurt." Cole's sole focus right now is me, his head bowed over our joined hands as he nurses my injury.

Marie's eyes widen as she watches Cole soothe my burned skin.

"I'm okay." I give her a reassuring smile. "Just a small boo-boo."

Marie smiles back at me, her curls bobbing as she nods her head. I watch her waddle back to the table and stifle a chuckle as she steals her brother's toast.

"This isn't small," Cole grumbles. "You're lucky it's not worse than this." He raises those storm eyes to mine when I snort. "What?"

I shrug. "I never thought you'd be the mother hen type."

Cole lets my hand slip from his as he straightens, our hands dripping with water. "You're not used to someone taking care of you, are you? And you said it yourself last night. I go above and beyond for the people I care for."

I'm stunned silent.

I've been independent my entire adult life, running around, making deals. No one's taken care of me besides me. Or rather, I've never let someone take care of me. That's my job and I do it well.

Until I didn't.

My mouth opens, but I'm not sure what to say. He sees right through me and he knows it.

Those storm eyes brighten like the clouds parting after a squall. "Don't worry," he says with a soft smile, gathering napkins and wiping up my soaked hand. "I'm used to taking care of people. I'm more than happy to add you to my list." Then, like the suave lawyer that he is, he leaves me standing there dumbfounded.

I'm still trying to wrap my mind around the exchange through our hectic morning. Cole tried to talk me through the schedule during breakfast, but my addled brain wasn't having it.

Plus, the kids were acting up. Jett hit Marie for stealing his bacon, Marie bit him in retaliation before Jett pushed her off her seat.

They both have their fair share of injuries. Poor Jett has a bruising mark on his forearm in the shape of his sister's teeth. She's a spunky little one, that's for sure. Marie bonked her chin on the way down and bit her lip leaving behind a small cut on her bottom lip.

It seems like the only person making it through the day unscathed is Cole.

Cool, calm, collected Cole.

Except...

His mouth's set into a thin, tense line. The muscle in his jaw clenches rhythmically the closer we get to the venue for the rehearsal. We've been so focused on the kids and them getting to see their mother that I haven't stopped to think about how Cole's handling all of this.

It must be difficult. Bringing your children to see the mother who left them and never looked back. Who left you and didn't think twice.

And now he's here, trailing behind their children as they run down the sidewalk, his hands clenched into fists, his shoulders tight and square, while their smiles and laughter are contagious.

Not for the first time, a sense of admiration for him settles through me. He's faced so many challenges. Overcome the hardships of single fatherhood that were thrust on his broad shoulders, and still, even now, he's showing up for his children.

His eyes are glued to Marie's bouncing curls, the Florida humidity working its magic on them, as she toddles behind her brother. Jett turns, shouting and waving at him, gaining a tight smile before a stern expression takes back over his handsome face.

If there's anything I can do to make any of this easier for him, I'll do it. He deserves that much.

The Sunshine State might be the death of me. Although the weather threw a wrench in our travel plans, it doesn't seem to have caused any damage. All it left behind was some debris and a lot of humidity.

I feel like a melting snowman. Hair sticks to my face and neck. Sweat pools in places that I didn't know sweat belonged in. What I wouldn't give for a slight breeze to lift the light fabric of my dress for just a hint of relief from the chaffing happening between my thighs.

Jett slows, sweat gathering at his temples. "Are we almost there? I'm hot."

"At least I'm not the only one dying," I mumble, squinting my eyes against the late-afternoon sun.

Cole chuckles, shooting a look at me before digging his phone out of his pocket to check the location. "It should be right around the corner," he shouts. "Wait right there for us."

A distant 'okay' drifts to us as Jett takes a seat in the shade of the Spanish moss-covered tree.

"All that fuss about his clothes and he's going to get grass stains on 'em before we even get there," I complain.

After our chaotic breakfast, we went out and did some exploring and shopping before heading back to the hotel for a quick nap time. Jett refused to sleep, but Marie and I cuddled up in my room and conked out. Cole woke us up an hour before we had to leave, which was quickly followed by Jett's tantrum about having to wear nice clothes.

Cole sighs, shaking his head in sympathy. "That's a five-year-old for ya."

Marie trips over her feet, catching herself before falling. She pushes herself up before either of us can react, tossing a smile over her shoulder, and taking off again.

I smile, watching the two kids that have wiggled their way into my heart. Even after all the craziness of the last two days, I wouldn't trade a single moment with them for anything.

Just as Cole said, the venue peeks out from around the curve.

Marie grabs my hand as we walk up the steps to the elegant venue.

Nerves for all three of them swirl in my stomach. Nothing about this situation has anything to do with me, but somehow I'm more nervous now than if I was about to make a large acquisition.

Cole holds open the large glass doors for us, his hand falling to the small of my back as he ushers us inside the air-conditioned room.

A small part of me —okay, not so small part—doesn't want him to let go and a tinge of disappointment stings through me when he does.

It takes a moment for my eyes to adjust from the brightness of the outdoors to the dim, romantic lighting of the room.

Edison lights hang from old wood beams, wisteria and Spanish moss hanging amongst it, giving the entire room an otherworldly feel to it.

Marie, Jett, and I have our eyes glued to the ceiling, various stages of awe making their way out of our mouths, but Cole isn't.

The warmth of the man I know evaporates, replaced by the cold steel of the lawyer. "Camilla."

Oh shit.

I mean, I knew she had to be gorgeous to snag Cole, but damn. Camilla is a beauty. Thick, dark hair curls down to her waist, her dark eyes alluring in the soft lighting. Her skin practically glows, all golden tan.

Jett stiffens as she walks towards us, her arms outstretched. "Jett."

His trepidation isn't what I expected. His wide blue eyes shoot to me, then behind my shoulder to his dad, before flitting back to Camilla.

"Are you gonna go say hi, son?" Cole's gentle encouragement is all he needs. He walks into his mother's arms, where she's crouched in front of him.

As happy as I am for Jett, I can't help but feel hurt for Cole. Marie's hand grips mine as I turn my gaze to Cole, more worried about how he's handling it all. A soft smile lines his face as he watches his son reunite with the mother who left.

Without meaning to, my free hand drifts back, offering him a hand to hold in this moment. Sapphire blue eyes meet mine a split second before the warmth of this palm brushes against my skin.

Camilla kisses Jett on the cheek before standing. "Where's my little girl?"

Cole's grip tightens.

Giving him a reassuring squeeze back, I lean down to where Marie grips my other hand. "Wanna go see her?"

Marie hides her face in my dress, untangling our hands to grab my thigh to hide behind. For the second time today, she's got her arms locked around my leg, but there's no way I'm going to make her let go.

"It's okay," I whisper to her. "You can stay with me."

A golden, delicate hand stretches out to me. "Hi, I'm Camilla. It's nice to meet you." Her gaze lingers on where Marie buries her face in my leg. While I understand her hurt, I won't betray the trust of this little girl.

"Joanna," I say with a smile. I can't help but stare at the giant, glistening diamond on her left hand where it's wrapped around Jetts.

"Joanna," she repeats, sounding preoccupied. Her gaze finally meets mine before drifting to Cole. "Thank you for bringing them. It means a lot." Her eyes widen when she sees Cole's hand in mine. I can see the question on her face before she even asks it. "Are you Cole's girlfriend?"

My mind whirrs. Like an old computer being rebooted, the forgotten gears start turning. I'm back in my element, in a fast-paced, quick decision making realm—an almost long-forgotten skill by now.

I said I wanted to make this easier for Cole in whatever way I could. I think I just found a way.

"N—"

"Yes," I blurt before Cole can finish contradicting me. His wide, confused gaze flicks to mine before narrowing with suspicion. I turn my attention back to his ex-wife, giving her a dazzling grin. "For almost a year now. Right, babe?"

Cole clears his throat, stepping closer behind me. His chest presses against my back as he drops my hand to wrap his arm around my waist.

As if all the air is sucked out of the room, my breath turns heavy and shallow.

"That's right."

Chapter Ten

Cole

My jaw aches, my palms itch, and my heart pounds. My ex-wife's wedding rehearsal was the last place I thought I'd fight the reaction my body has to Joanna, but here I am.

She smiles politely, her curvy body tucked comfortably against my side, completely unaware of the effect she has on me.

I've dreamed about having my hands on her body. Longed to have her in my arms, face flushed, and body willing.

Holding myself back from doing all the things I've wanted to do since I saw her that day in the grocery store is proving more difficult than I imagined.

Especially now, with my daughter clinging to her. With my ex-wife introducing herself to the woman who has helped pull me out from the sea I was drowning under.

The woman I know I'm falling for.

"Where are my grandchildren?" The familiar accented voice of my former mother-in-law pushes aside my racing thoughts about Joanna.

It's easy to overlook Maria. She's a tiny woman, not even five feet tall, with a kind face and even kinder heart. The resemblance between my daughter and the older woman currently making her way up the steps is unmistakable.

Jett's face lights up. He wrenches his hand free from his mother's and runs to his abuela.

She hugs Jett tightly, raining kisses on his cheeks, his laughter jubilant.

Maria has been an unshakable pillar since Camilla left. The effort she makes each week to be a part of my children's lives is endearing. Weekly video calls and check-ins have kept her involved even while being hundreds of miles away.

Marie gasps, her brown eyes flicking between me and her grandmother as if asking for permission.

"Go on," I say gently to Marie, where she clutches Joanna's dress.

She doesn't let go of Joanna's dress until the last moment, reaching for her grandmother with a dazzling smile.

I don't bother looking at Camilla. I'm too busy enjoying this moment, one that was a deciding factor in making this journey.

Joanna's gaze burns against my skin. She smiles, looking between the four of us.

Maria adjusts Marie on her hip, extending her hand. "You must be Joanna," she says with a smile. "I've heard a lot about you."

They exchange pleasantries before Maria turns to me, pulling me into a hug. I don't dare let go of Joanna, not now that I have her close.

"I'm glad you made it," she whispers into my ear before pulling back, her smile soft.

"Welcome, everyone." Feedback from the speakers has guests turning towards the small stage. "If you would, we are ready to start the rehearsal. Please make your way through the double doors at the back so we can get started."

Camilla reaches for Jett's hand, leading him through the crowd, her fiance meeting them halfway.

"I'll keep an eye on them." Joanna pulls away, but I tighten my grip on her hip.

Maria waves her off. "Don't you worry about it. Let me watch my nietos. You two relax." Marie clutches her grandmother's dress.

"Are you sure? I can—"

"It's fine," I whisper into her ear, drowning in the scent of her intoxicating perfume.

Joanna's spine straightens and she shivers. "Alright."

I turn to Maria. "Thank you." She gives a smile and a knowing nod, picking up my daughter and leaving me alone with Joanna.

There's so much I want to say. Unspoken words and thoughts drift to the surface.

"Joanna—"

She steps out of my grasp, her cheeks flushed. "I'm going to the ladies' room."

Joanna leaves me standing there, watching her walk away.

I'm even more speechless than I was two seconds ago.

Her hips sway enticingly as she sneaks down the dark hall to the restroom. The sky blue dress hugs her every curve before flowing down to her knee.

Questions race through my head. Why did she do this? Did she mean it? What does it mean?

For months I've been toeing the boundary I built the moment she showed up on my porch. And I'm no saint. I'm damn near ready to ignite the dynamite and blow the whole fucking wall down.

My gaze lingers down the hallway she disappeared down. I want to follow her. Press her for answers to my questions.

Last night, there was a shift between us. I felt it then, baring my past to her. Maybe something else has shifted too. Something I've been longing for ever since I saw her in that grocery aisle.

A muffled voice from the microphone slips through the wall of glass as the rehearsal starts. Maria stands at the back, Marie on her hip and Jett at her side.

Aside from the staff setting up catering and the bartender, I'm all alone.

We could be alone.

I need answers. I need to know if she's feeling what I'm feeling, too.

With determined strides, I slip down the hall and lean against the wall opposite the door, praying like hell I don't fuck this up.

It's not long before the bathroom door whooshes open. Curled tendrils of hair framing her face float around her like she's an angel. Her eyes are downcast, not noticing me until we're practically face to face.

"Oh my god," she gasps. "You scared me." A hand flies to her chest over her racing heart. Sweet perfume floods my nostrils and I take an involuntary step forward.

"Sorry. Wasn't my intention." I hold my hands up innocently.

She chuckles, waving me off. "Everything okay?"

Is everything okay? We made it to Florida. My kids reunited with their mother. Get to spend time with their grandmother. But the one thing that isn't okay is the feelings I have for her.

I shake my head. "No."

"Oh." Her face falls. Sharp eyes scan down my body before landing back on my face. "What is it? Do I need to throat punch somebody?"

I snort, unable to stop my smile from spreading. "You might."

Joanna leans against the wall next to me. "What's up, counselor?"

"What are we doing, Joanna?"

Her lips part as she sucks in a breath. "What do you mean?"

The way she's looking at me right now tells me she knows exactly what I mean.

My palm lifts to cup her face. "Why did you lie?"

Joanna shudders, her eyes slipping closed. Gone is the lighthearted humor from a minute ago. The air between us grows thick.

She swallows before those blue eyes meet mine. "I know today sucks for you, and I don't want to see you upset. I wanted to make it better in any way that I could. I'm sorry if I made it worse."

I can't stop myself from reaching for her. Her back presses against the wall, my hand on her waist. "You've never made anything worse." My voice is soft, the truth of my words shining through. "You've only ever made things better. Can't you see that?"

Her breath quickens, her hand reaching up to press against my chest, the heat of her small touch burning my skin.

The air seems to boil around us, crackling with intensity. I squeeze her waist, letting my hand slip from her cheek to run along her exposed collarbone. Over her pounding pulse and back to her reddened cheek. Velvet smooth skin glides along my palm, the feel of her becoming my new addiction.

I'm just as breathless as she is, and the way her gaze slides from my eyes to my lips?

Fuck, I want to kiss her.

She nods, her teeth scraping along her full bottom lip. "Yes."

My thumb traces the small indentations her teeth made, completely entranced by the way her lips part beneath my touch. Her hot breath glides over my thumb, all my attention locked on her tempting mouth. Every instinct is screaming at me to bridge the gap, to close the space between us and press my lips against hers.

But I can't. Not until I know she wants it, too.

"I have one more question, and I need you to answer honestly."

She nods. "Okay."

I swallow hard, my thumb tracing the soft skin under her lip. "Tell me I'm not alone in feeling this. Tell me you've been fighting whatever this is between us, too."

Joanna tilts her chin towards mine, our lips mere inches apart. Her voice is barely a whisper as she says, "You're not alone."

"Good." I take one last look down at her, my eyes sliding down her body before lingering on her lips. I lick mine as if to pacify the urge to feel hers.

Voices echo from the end of the hall, growing louder each second.

I sigh, frustration making me clench my jaw. My thumb runs once more against her parted lips. "Later."

Joanna gapes at me as I slide my hands off her body and leave her standing in the hallway.

Chapter Eleven

Joanna

"What do you mean 'nothing else happened'?" Hazel tosses her wild hair over her shoulder and adjusts her sunglasses.

It's been a whirlwind of a weekend. We're all exhausted and dragging our feet. Everyone except little miss Marie.

The chains of the swing set squeak with each push. After going to Florida, we needed to get back into our normal routine. Marie claps her hands, her smile wide and face joyful.

I laugh at the incredulous look Hazel shoots my way. She couldn't wait to hear what happened on our trip that she met us at the park for her lunch. "Don't look at me like that. It's not like we had a lot of alone time."

"Not even a little smooch?" She puckers her lips, making kissing noises and leaning down to Marie as she swings back and forth. Marie lets out an adorable squealing laugh.

We're very aware of the little ears constantly listening to everything.

"No, not even a smooch," I chuckle. "We talked a lot. Flirted more than a lot." A flush creeps up my neck.

We left the rehearsal early, walking hand-in-hand back to the car. Picked up some hamburgers for dinner and ate in the rooms.

My heart pounds even now thinking about the way he looked at me. Collar open, the sleeves of his dress shirt rolled up to his elbows, the hint of skin at the base of his neck. He didn't hide the desire behind his eyes, that flash of heat I would sometimes find there.

I didn't hide mine either.

But, as much as I wanted to finish what he started in the hallway, it wasn't the time. All we were left with were lingering glances and innocent touches, the graze of a hand, a palm on my back.

Even those small moments of his skin against mine had my breath hitching and pulse pounding.

Later can't come soon enough.

Jett, Marie, and I went to the wedding the next day. Cole dropped us off and went back to the hotel. If I were him, I wouldn't want to be at my ex-wife's wedding either.

I pretend not to notice the picture I took of the three of us smiling on the dance floor as his lock screen on his phone.

We left early yesterday morning like we planned. Both kids were still sleeping when we strapped them into their car seats, pajamas and all.

Hazel waves her hand in a circle. "You can't leave me hanging like that. C'mon, what'd you talk about?"

I shrug. "Everything. Stories from growing up. Us." Somewhere along the way, I think we both realized that what started in that hallway can't be stopped. Only when the car grew quiet from sleeping kids did we talk about our feelings for one another and how this will work between us. "We're keeping it quiet for now, but there's definitely an *us*."

Hazel's face lights up. "Well, I'm proud of you. I'm surprised you listened to me for once. It's nice to know my meddling paid off."

I snort. "It was bound to happen at some point."

Once Marie has her fill of swinging, we eat our packed lunches, catching up on what I missed while we were gone.

"I'm going to have...drumroll please..." Marie and I thrum our hands against the picnic table. "A niece!"

"It's a girl!" Marie glances up at me, confused. She claps, letting out a "yay" before reaching for her applesauce pouch. "I'm so excited for them."

"Me too. Think of all the cute girly outfits I'll get to buy. Not that I hate all the tractors and dinosaur stuff I get for Mason, but I'm ready for rainbows and unicorns."

"And princesses," I add. "Can't forget about those."

"Pin-cess," Marie agrees.

Marie finishes eating and takes off for the jungle gym. Hazel and I follow closely behind, chatting while she plays.

Before long, it's time to pack up. Marie angrily kicks her little legs when I pull her from the jungle gym not ready to leave. She's tired though, and after some cajoling, she settles into the stroller.

"Oh, I forgot to tell you something. I don't know how I forgot," she chastises, shaking her head. "Grant and I watched Tristan this weekend."

"Is that a secret?" I chuckle. It's the busy season for Wells' landscaping company, and it's not unusual for Grant to watch Tristan.

Hazel ignores me. "Tristan mentioned Wells has a 'friend.'" She uses air quotes. "I tried to get him to tell me more, but you know how it is trying to keep a five-year-old on topic."

"A friend, huh? Interesting." There's not a lot I know about Wells. He's more mysterious than Cole and Grant.

"I know. Grant tells me to leave it alone, but I want more info."

We've reached the parking lot and head to Hazel's car. "I'm sure we'll find out soon enough. The guys can't keep anything to themselves for long."

Hazel laughs. "Isn't that the truth?" She pulls me in for a quick hug before bending down to wave bye to Marie.

The soft vibration of the wheels on concrete, coupled with tiring play time, lulls Marie to sleep.

It doesn't take us long to round the corner of our street and I almost stop in my tracks.

Cole's sleek SUV sits in the driveway.

My heart hammers in my chest. Nerves and anticipation gather in my stomach. Each step closer to the house acts like kindling to the flame.

I'm sure there's a perfectly logical reason for Cole to be home. But that doesn't stop my imagination from taking over.

Marie snores softly in her stroller, and instead of risking waking her up with the garage, I push her up the path leading to the front door.

Picking up a sleeping toddler from their stroller without waking them up is a newly learned skill. Marie's hot cheek presses into the hollow of my shoulder, a bit of drool cooling my skin.

The door opens before I reach for the handle.

Cole gives me that crooked smile I love before silently ushering me inside. The thumb on the hand he places on my lower back rubs tantalizing circles. That all too familiar heat floods through me, pooling right between my thighs.

He looks way too good today. The blue button-down shirt is open, exposing a delicious expanse of skin. His typical business jacket is nowhere to be seen, likely tossed on the back of the couch.

My mouth dries by looking at him.

Based on the smirk he gives me, he knows it, too.

Plastic and metal click together as he folds down the stroller, closing the door before setting it in the entryway.

As much as I want to know why he's home, I need to get Marie into bed.

It's hard to climb up steps when you can't see them, so I take my time. Long enough for Cole to catch up to me. My breath hitches as his hand rests at the small of my back, guiding me up the last few steps.

Does he know how each touch is torture? That I want him to touch more than my back, or graze his hand against mine? Can he feel the need too?

That touch doesn't fade even when we step into Marie's room and I place her in her bed.

I back away as Cole lowers himself down, whispering soft words to his daughter before kissing her reddened cheek.

In the hallway, my heart races in my chest.

Cole's home early. He's here and I don't know why, and I'm losing my mind. Those small touches guiding me up the stairs have sent me spiraling.

The house passes by in my periphery. With Marie asleep, Cole and I are alone. In this house. Together.

The last time we were alone, he pushed me against the wall. Made a promise of later.

I'm all worked up, and he hasn't even said one word to me.My hands tremble as I unload the remnants of our lunch. Soft footsteps pad on the hardwood floor.

My eyes slip closed as Cole's warm hands slide across my shoulders before wrapping around my waist. His hot body brackets mine against the kitchen island. Anticipation swirls through me, my breath hitching as his warm breath tickles against my neck.

We're both breathing heavily as lips brush against my skin. My body turns to jello and I sink back against him, his hard body melding with my soft curves.

It's the second time he's pressed his body against mine like this. The only difference is this time, I want him more.

Every nerve ending tingles with the need for him to touch me, kiss me. Hell, do *anything*.

"Joanna." The deep rumble of his voice sends chills through me and my pussy clenches.

I swallow. "Cole."

Slowly, he presses his lips against my neck. Each kiss throws sparks of heat through me, flowing from my limbs and pooling in my belly. "Do you know what you do to me?" He blows out a breath that's almost a chuckle. "I left a meeting early because I needed to see you. Feel you. Talk to you. You're driving me out of my mind."

Everything from this weekend boils to the surface. Every glance. Every touch. The trace of his thumb across my lips. The warmth of his hand on my waist.

But it's more than that.

The way he makes me laugh. How he loves his children. His caring, thoughtful nature. The way he's dedicated to being the best father and man he can be. Not because it's asked of him, but because he chooses it. He doesn't take the easy route. Faces things head on and pushes forward.

I turn in his arms, wanting to get lost in the deep blue of his irises.

Cole steps closer, pushing me back against the counter. "I can't stop thinking about you," he whispers. "You've been on my mind since that day in the cereal aisle. I looked for you. Made us walk the entire store trying to find you. I would've gone back the next week and the next just to learn your name."

I cup his face. "You did?"

He nods, my favorite smile pulling at the lips I dream about. "Jett was complaining that his feet hurt by the time we left."

This time I'm the one brushing my thumb against his lips. Those eyes slip closed like he's keeping himself from wanting more. His lips are hot and smooth, and so soft. "I thought about you every day," I admit. "I've wanted you since before I stepped on your porch."

The truth of our words lies heavy between us.

It's terrifying and exhilarating.

All the reasons this shouldn't happen disappear when he looks at me. Heat simmers in the sapphire depths of his gaze.

Cole's looking at me like I'm the beginning and the end. "Are you sure about this? I know we talked about it, but..." The words linger between us. Even now, he's giving me time to choose. He sucks in a steady breath and whispers, "I won't do anything to lose you." His eyes glance up at the ceiling, towards his sleeping daughter above us. "We can't lose you. Even if it means never touching you again."

The choice between heartbreak and happiness rests in my hands. And I've already chosen.

Chapter Twelve

Joanna

We're two rubber bands pulled too tight, snapping and recoiling back to the only place that makes sense.

Months of repressed attraction and desperate longing released with a single brush of our lips.

Cole's hand fists around my ponytail holding me to him as our lips finally touch. Fire ignites in my veins, flames growing hotter from the deep moan Cole makes as my tongue slides against his.

I'm a reckless mess. Deserting all sense of normalcy and professionalism, but Cole's right there with me.

The kiss is deep and powerful, rocking me down to my core. This volcano between us is erupting and I'm damn near ready to throw myself into it.

Cole pulls back. "I've wanted to do that for a long time."

I run my hand across his cheek. "So why didn't you?"

He captures my hand, kissing my palm. "I wasn't sure." My favorite grin crosses his lips. "But now I am."

Without giving me time to breathe, Cole devours me. This kiss? It's the kind that leaves a lasting impression.

All care and worry cease to exist.

He's not my boss.

I'm not his nanny.

We're two people drawn together with an intense need.

Cole effortlessly lifts me onto the cold marble of kitchen island. I wrap my legs around his waist, pulling him closer to me.

This is what I dreamed about after our kitchen run-in. To feel his warmth. Taste his lips.

I've become possessed with the need to have him.

Cole grips my hips and rocks me into him. His growing erection presses deliciously against my pounding clit and I moan.

"Fuck. Joanna." He tugs off my jacket, kissing along my neck and shoulders.

I unbutton his shirt, sliding my fingers along his chest. We find a rhythm, the growing friction making me moan.

It's the most intense, exquisite, sensual moment of my life. I never want it to end.

"I want you," I whisper between wanton breaths.

Cole's low moan sends shivers down my spine and goosebumps along my skin. He kisses his way up to my lips, his hands tugging on the waist of my jeans. "Joanna—"

But he's not pulling them off.

Instead, Cole scoops me up. A surprised peep from me has him laughing against the sensitive skin of my neck, the vibration sending shock waves through me. "I wonder what other sounds I can drag out of you."

Those simple words have my muscles clenching in anticipation. "I didn't peg you as a dirty talker. Maybe you're all talk and no action, counselor."

He's not taking me upstairs. No, he's carrying me further into the house, and farther away from a sleeping Marie.

"You're about to find out."

This time, I'm the one laughing. "Promises, promises."

The depths of his blue eyes sparkle and shine with heat, mischief, desire.

I know he sees the same in mine.

He takes us through the kitchen and down the short hallway that leads to the laundry room and his office. The door to his office creaks open. Leather bound law books line the shelves behind his expensive looking desk.

Instead of taking me to the couch tucked into the corner, he sets me on the edge of his desk. He towers over me, his eyes trailing down my body. "I need to know that you're okay with this." Cole cups my face, his thumb tracing my lips tauntingly.

I wrap an arm around his waist, sincerity filling every word. "You won't lose me. You've buried yourself in my heart, right along with Jett and Marie. I'm never letting you go."

The words barely leave my mouth before they're silenced by his lips. Everything is let loose. All boundaries dissolve into an invisible heap on the floor.

Exactly where they'll stay.

My stomach tightens with anticipation, my whole body aching for his touch. For too long, I've waited for it, and now that I have it, I want more.

Steady hands methodically work to rid me of my clothes, pull my hair free, caress my breasts. He's barely touched me, and I'm a panting, writhing mess. I can feel the wetness pooling between my thighs, my clit pounding, my pussy clenching around nothing.

"Wait," I gasp as Cole sucks his way down my neck.

Cole pulls back, his eyes wide. "Are you okay?"

"No. You have on more clothes than me."

He releases a breath. "By all means," he steps back, "don't let me stop you."

Cole watches me intensely. His breath hitches, hands squeeze my hips, pulsing with impatience. He lets me take my time, though. Lets me run my hands down his torso, marveling at the ridges of his abdomen, kiss the place above his heart, unbuckle his belt.

I bite my lip, sucking in a breath as Cole gasps, my hand stroking over his hard cock. Enamored, I do it again, loving the hitch in his breath, the way his eyes shutter closed.

He doesn't let me have my fun for long.

Large hands grab mine. "My turn."

Cole doesn't take his time, nor do I want him to. Hair flops onto his forehead as he kneels between my bare thighs. The only thing separating my pussy from his mouth is my cotton panties.

Slowly, deliberately, Cole purses his lips and blows. The stark contrast between his cool breath and my overheated skin makes me gasp. He chuckles. "I like that sound."

I'm breathless, on edge, and desperate for more. "If you keep going, you'll hear way more."

"Will I?" He drags my panties down my thighs, and I lift my hips, helping him until my bare ass sits on his desk. "Let's find out."

His eyes never leave mine as he lifts my legs over his shoulder and spreads my thighs. My heart races, my muscles clenching around nothing. He takes his time, blowing against my clit and watching me squirm.

"You have no idea how many times I've thought about you like this. Spread wide and ready for me."

Cole's the picture of restraint. His hands slide around my thighs, up to my waist. He doesn't balk at my rolls or the faint stretch marks tracing across my hips. He's slow. Deliberate. Maddening.

By the time he lowers his mouth to the apex of my thighs, I'm more than ready.

Heat envelopes my center. My eyes slip closed, relishing the slide of his tongue along my folds. My back hits the flat surface of Cole's desk with a dull thump. I use his shoulders as leverage, my hips grinding my pussy against his face. A rumbling moan of satisfaction sends a shock of vibration against my clit, my strangled cry filling the room.

Finally, his restraint snaps.

Cole nips at my thigh, groaning in frustration. "Fuck, Joanna. You have no idea what you're doing to me." He stands, stepping out of his remaining clothes. I watch him with lust-filled eyes, not bothering to hide my wandering gaze.

I sit up, wrapping my hand around his cock. "I need you."

Cole's warm breath skates over my skin, his hands brushing my hair away from my face. "Are you sure about this?" Even as he's asking for permission, he grips my hips, dragging me closer to the edge. Closer to him.

A humourless laugh bubbles up my throat. I inhale his scent, placing teasing kisses at the base of his neck. "I'm sitting naked on your desk. Your face is wet from my pussy, my hand's around your cock, and you think I'm not sure?" I squeeze his cock and his hips jerk.

"Joanna." My name on his lips spurs me on. I wrap my legs around his hips, rubbing his cock through my wet pussy, and notching him at my opening.

Eternity lies in this moment between us. Our chests brush. My lips part against his as he lavishes me with a passionate kiss.

With one quick thrust, Cole pushes into me, stealing my breath. He hisses a curse, his fingers digging deliciously into my hips.

For months we've danced around each other, both of us fighting against this. But now we're letting go of everything we've been holding back.

I moan as he starts to move. Cole takes his time to savor me. For me to savor him. My hands run up his shoulders before trailing down to his hips. Cole does the same, brushing my hair out of my face before kissing my lips.

Pleasure builds slowly with each thrust of his hips. It's intense and deep, and it's almost too much to bear.

"Faster, please," I gasp.

He moans, burying his head in the crook of my neck before he rocks into me at a maddening pace. I'm surrounded by him, wrapped in his embrace. Whispered words of praise send tingles down my spine.

My breath hitches, the intense pleasure coiling like a snake waiting to strike.

"Are you close, Joanna?" Cole's words send jolts of pleasure straight to my pussy. I moan, my muscles tensing around him. "Fuck, you're so tight. So perfect."

"Yes," say between panting breaths. My body is under his control, dangling over the edge and waiting to fall.

He slides his hands under my ass, tilting my hips. He plunges even deeper, hitting a sensitive spot. A sound I've never heard scrapes up my throat. I clutch him to me, lost in the intense sensation.

"Come on, Joanna," he pants, picking up speed. "Let me feel you."

Again and again he hits that spot. I'm lost to everything except the pleasure.

"That's it. Feel it. Come on, Joanna." Cole fists my hair, titling my chin up. Teeth scrape against my jaw, his tongue flicking along my skin. "Let go."

Like a spring let loose, my orgasm snaps. I cry out as my body spasms. Tears slip down my cheeks at the intensity of my climax. Cole never stops murmuring words of praise through gritted teeth.

His control is slipping.

He never stops his blistering pace, working me through my orgasm and drawing him closer to his. I deliberately squeeze around him with each thrust, wanting to see him let loose.

"Cole," I moan.

With a guttural groan, Cole comes. He clutches me to him, his chest heaving. His whole body shakes against mine and a feeling of contentment settles inside of me.

I've never known happiness like this.

For years, I thought my life was meant to be busy. Constantly going after the next best thing. But in these past months, my life has changed for the better.

I might not know what's coming next, but I know I'll spend it with Cole and his children at my side.

Epilogue One

Cole

Three Weeks Later

"We need something to hold the balloons down." Grant struggles with the bundle of pink balloons in his grip. Wind gusts sending leaves—and the balloons—fluttering.

The corner of the princess tablecloths lifts and I throw myself on it to keep it from blowing away.

An outdoor birthday party during fall maybe wasn't the best decision, but what Marie wants, Marie gets. For the most part.

"There should be weights in one of the bags." I gesture toward the plastic bags flapping in the breeze Hazel and Joanna packed, sitting solidly on the ground.

Joanna's been working tirelessly to put together my daughter's third birthday party. Every day I'd come home to bags of decorations, balloon kits, and excited stories from Marie about their day. I might not have understood everything she said, but her enthusiasm was clear.

Grant searches through the bags, locating the weights. Together, we secure the balloons, scouting for nearby rocks to avoid a balloon disaster.

"Is that everything?" Grant places his hands on his hips surveying our hard work.

It looks like Barbie's dream house threw up.

Pink balloons, streamers, tablecloths, cupcakes, pink everything.

"Looks like it."

"Dad!" Jett and Harrison come running through the park, Hazel, Joanna, and Marie following behind them. "Can we go play?"

Grant gives them permission and they take off. We picked the picnic tables next to the jungle gym for a reason. The kids can wear themselves out while we watch them from a close distance.

"Wow, you guys did great." Hazel gives Grant a quick peck. "I'm amazed."

Marie runs straight to me and I scoop her up. "Do you like it?"

Her eyes widen. "My crown!"

"Yes," I laugh, carrying her to the table where the princess crown she picked out sits. "You wanna put it on?"

Joanna hands me the crown, our fingers touching for the briefest of moments. It doesn't matter that it's been an hour since I've seen her. No touch is enough.

We've been keeping our relationship quiet for now. Although with the winks Hazel shoots my way, I have a feeling she already knows.

Meaning Grant knows too. But he hasn't once brought it up, and I'm thankful for that. I want to keep Joanna to myself for a bit longer.

"Beautiful." Joanna smiles at my beaming daughter. "Let's take a picture. Say cheese!"

Marie obliges, letting out a word similar to cheese, but not quite. "I see," she demands, reaching for Joanna.

Watching Joanna and Marie interact never ceases to amaze me. She's grown so much thanks to Joanna's loving comfort and I'll spend my life thanking the woman who transformed our lives for the better.

"Hey, Cole, can I get your help? We left some stuff in the trunk." Joanna sets Marie on her feet.

I nod. "Sure."

We leave Grant and Hazel to watch the kids, and head to the parking lot.

Once we're far enough away, I slide my hand into hers. The last thing we want to do is confuse the kids, so for now, we take these moments when we can get them.

It feels like I'm a teenager again. Sneaking around the house. Whispering behind closed doors. "Helping" Joanna do laundry simply so I can sneak in a kiss.

I bring our linked hands to my mouth, kissing her hand. "You look beautiful."

Joanna laughs. "Thank you. Your daughter had some strong feelings about my outfit. She wanted me to wear a dress to match hers."

The light pink dress blows slightly in the wind, and Joanna plants a hand against her thigh to keep it in place.

"She does love dresses. I don't mind that she keeps making you wear them. I love seeing you in leggings but dresses?"

Joanna leans against the car. "Really? Does that do it for you?"

"You do it for me." I lean down, kissing her perfect lips.

She moans before pulling back. "Good."

I grip her hips, loving the feel of her in my arms. "Is there something we need to get, or was this an excuse to get me alone?"

She scoffs. "Of course there is."

Both of our hands are full of presents on the way back to the picnic area. Joanna struggles to keep her dress down, but I don't mind the quick flash of her thighs, as long as no one else sees.

It doesn't take long for Marie's friends to show up. Little girls from her dance class give her hugs before they take off to play.

Joanna and Hazel chat with the moms, laughing as they watch the girls play.

My life has turned completely upside down. Since we met each other in that cereal aisle, not a day has gone by without thinking about her.

She's the woman of my dreams.

"Um, are you seeing what I'm seeing?" Grant nudges my shoulder.

My eyes snap to the jungle gym, searching for our sons. They're chasing each other on the bridge, large smiles across their faces. "And what should I be seeing?"

"Who the hell is with Wells?"

"What?" I choke. "Where?"

Grant nods toward the sidewalk. I scan the park for our friend, finally spotting him as he rounds the corner emerging from behind a tree.

It's a...woman.

Long black hair blows in the wind a step behind Wells. It's clear they're together. Wells barely takes his eyes off of her before offering his hand.

Grant shakes his head. "Are you seeing what I'm seeing?"

I blink, trying to justify what I'm seeing with my own two eyes. "I don't fucking believe it."

Find out what happens in
Desired By The Single Dad
Coming Soon

Epilogue Two

Joanna
One Year Later

Hot water pelts against my face. It's way too early to be awake, and I'm feeling the effects of our late night.

Grant and Hazel took the kids for the night, and Cole and I made good use of our time together. Life has been busy, and since I've started a new job at a small business here in town, finding time to focus on just the two of us has been hard.

Marie started pre-school this year, and I wanted something to do with my extra time. It's only part-time during school hours, but it keeps me busy. Cole's supportive, even though I think he secretly misses me being "his nanny."

It was fun sneaking around. Sexy even.

We had officially been together for several months before we started to be more open with our relationship in front of the kids. Jett asked some questions, ones that made me giggle and earned a scathing look from Cole, but Jett just shrugged and kept playing like we hadn't told him that his daddy's in love with his nanny.

It didn't take long for me to move down the hall into Cole's room. More often than not, I'd end up sleeping in his bed, waking up to Jett's feet in my face and Marie's knobby knees digging into my side.

We've created our little family, even if it's unorthodox.

The glass doors to our shower clicks open. "Good morning."

Cole's naked, sweaty chest rests against my back as he pulls me against him. "Good morning." I turn in his arms, kissing him softly. "Did you have a good run?"

He smiles that crooked grin, his hands squeezing my ass. "Not as good as seeing you naked."

My laugh is cut off with a breath-taking kiss. The hunger and urgency in it makes me moan.

This never gets old. We spent the night wrapped in each other, yet the feeling of his lips against mine still sends shivers down my spine.

Cold tiles press against my back, and I gasp. Water splatters off Cole's shoulders and he curses. "How the hell can you stand under that?" He reaches for the knob, the water instantly cooling.

I run my fingers through his hair. "It's relaxing."

"Is it?" he asks, my favorite grin sliding across his face. "I can think of something more relaxing than that." Cole's hungry eyes linger on my tight nipples before his hot mouth sucks one into his mouth as his thumb traces circles around the other.

Wet hair slips through my fingers as I grasp him closer to me. My heartbeat pounds in my pussy, and I can already feel the wetness pooling there.

He releases my nipple with a pop. "I love you. Fuck, I love you so much."

His hands wander down my body before hooking under my thighs. In one quick motion, Cole lifts me, pinning me between the shower wall and his hard body.

I brush wet hair away from his face, staring down into the eyes I know better than my own. "I love you."

Cole kisses me deeply as he lowers me onto his cock. "I need you to come fast," he pants. "Jett's game is in thirty minutes."

"You're not my boss anymore," I tease.

A playful smack to my ass wipes any teasing away. "And you're not my nanny. You're the woman I love, and right now, I need to hear you scream. Need to feel that pussy squeeze me tight while you come."

His dirty words send tingling heat to my belly. My moans echo off the tile walls as Cole fucks me. The shower steams from both the hot water and our panting sighs.

Cole knows exactly how to work my body. Every kiss, touch, drags me closer to orgasm.

He grinds against me as he bottoms out. "Stop holding out on me. I can feel how close you are."

A hand snakes up my body, pinching my nipple, and I come, my pussy clenching around him just like he wanted.

"Thank fuck." He groans, burying his head in my neck and losing himself in his own release.

After several minutes, Cole sets me back on my feet, but never lets me go. He takes his time washing me. Heat still simmers beneath my skin at his simple touches.

Cole's done before I am, drying his body efficiently with his towel, leaving me to moisturize and dry my hair.

He's waiting for me. Sitting on the end of our bed, Cole watches me with a heated gaze looking every bit as delicious as he did the day we met. He stands, dragging me into him before kissing my lips.

It wasn't an easy road to happiness. Both of us struggled with our own battles before coming into each other's lives. We found each other in a time of need, desperate for anything that works. Desperate for each other.

I'll be forever grateful for those mimosas, a grocery list, and a screaming toddler.

Because this family—my family—is everything I need.

Thanks For Reading

I hope you enjoyed Nanny for the Single Dad!

It means so much to me that out of all the books available; you picked up one of mine. So, whether you loved it or hated it, at least you took a chance on me. Thank you.

If Nanny for the Single Dad was the first book of mine that you picked up, I hope you take your time to read through my collection. I've been at this writing thing for several years now and have completed series and several interconnected stand-alone books with plans on publishing more in the future.

Whenever I get an idea for a book or a storyline, the first thing that typically pops into my head is a single line or a vivid image of a scene. Every. Time. For Loved by the Single Dad, it was watching my nephew's soccer game—well, more like his soccer coach. For this book, it was driving hours to my sister's house. One of my favorite songs came on the radio. You know the kind. The one where you can't not sing along to in your private concert speeding down the interstate. I'm sure you know exactly which scene I'm referring to (because you definitely finished the book, right?)

Want to know more about Wells? His book Desired by the Single Dad will be coming soon and is up for pre-order now!

If you could, please take a moment to rate and review on Amazon, Goodreads, Instagram, or wherever you post reviews. As an indie author, ratings and reviews are the best way of getting my work out there for other people to read. A little goes a long way!

Don't forget to follow me on Instagram @authorsierrashipley and sign up for my newsletter to get freebies and see more details about my coming books!

Thank you for your support!

Until next time,

Sierra

About the Author

SIERRA SHIPLEY IS A born and raised Midwest girl. She spends her days with her lovable rescue pup, Trip, who constantly wants all the cuddles, and her lovable cat Aidas. Her ideal day is spent drinking coffee, reading, and dreaming.

Sierra has always wanted the romance she's read in books. Pair that with an active imagination and a love of creativity, and you get a writer!

Her goal is to create steamy, romantic stories with characters that people can relate to.